Her vision becar
tipped upside do
breathe. When s
was with a gulp.
had to cover her n_____ napkin.

'You must have a temperature,' she said over the square of linen. 'You're delirious.'

'You have everything to gain, nothing to lose.'

'Except Marla's friendship when she bans me from her life for deceiving her.'

'I'm betting she'll name their first girl child after you. If not...' his smile softened '...she'll understand. That's what friends do.'

Slowly Roxy set her napkin down. 'You'd really commit to walking me down the aisle in that dress?'

'It's for a good cause. Besides, there's such a thing as annulment.' His laugh was a little too quick. 'We're not talking for real here, Roxy, just a means to an end. We both agreed. Neither of us is after that kind of commitment.'

She blinked and felt her cheeks go warm. Well, of course that was what he'd meant. This proposition was another of his angles to get to where he—and in this case she—wanted to go.

'Was that a yes?' he asked.

She fr_____ Sh_____'dn't agree.

'Way

One Christmas long ago, **Robyn Grady** received a book from her big sister and immediately fell in love with Cinderella. Sprinklings of magic, deepest wishes come true—she was hooked! Picture books with glass slippers later gave way to romance novels and, more recently, the real-life dream of writing for Mills & Boon.

After a fifteen-year career in television, Robyn met her own modern-day hero. They live on Australia's Sunshine Coast with their three little princesses, two poodles, and a cat called Tinkie. She loves new shoes, worn jeans, lunches at Moffat Beach and hanging out with her friends on eHarlequin. Learn about her latest releases at www.robyngrady.com, and don't forget to say hi. She'd love to hear from you!

Recent titles by the same author:

EVERY GIRL'S SECRET FANTASY
NAUGHTY NIGHTS IN THE MILLIONAIRE'S MANSION
DEVIL IN A DARK BLUE SUIT
FIRED WAITRESS, HIRED MISTRESS

Did you know these are also available as eBooks?
Visit www.millsandboon.co.uk

THE WEDDING MUST GO ON

BY
ROBYN GRADY

MILLS
BOON

First published in Great Britain 2012
by Mills & Boon, an imprint of Harlequin (UK) Limited.
Harlequin (UK) Limited, Eton House, 18-24 Paradise Road,
Richmond, Surrey TW9 1SR

© Robyn Grady 2012

ISBN: 978 0 263 89327 4

Harlequin (UK) policy is to use papers that are natural, renewable and recyclable products and made from wood grown in sustainable forests. The logging and manufacturing process conform to the legal environmental regulations of the country of origin.

Printed and bound in Spain
by Blackprint CPI, Barcelona

THE WEDDING
MUST GO ON

CHAPTER ONE

THE worst possible person at the worst possible time.

Peeking through a gap in her back-room door, Roxanne Trammel admitted that looks weren't the problem. The guest waiting at her Sydney wedding salon's point-of-sale counter was over six feet tall, delectably masculine in demeanour and build…those lidded ice-blue eyes and coal-black hair would set any woman's heartbeat tripping a thousand to one, including her own.

Roxy wanted to shrivel up and die because she *knew* that man. Knew him and more. That she'd slipped into this wedding gown moments ago was only the icing. The not so funny punchline to a bad joke she'd sooner forget.

Out by the counter, a line creased between the dark slashes of Nate Sparks's brows before he caught the time on his Omega then rubbed the back of his neck…the same strong neck Roxy had clung to with such fervour that fateful spring evening when they'd shared their first and only kiss. If she closed her eyes, she could still smell his woodsy scent…feel the graze of his sandpaper jaw along her cheek. The magic his touch stirred deep inside had transported her to another time. Another place. She could admit that she hadn't wanted that kiss to end.

But it had, and in the most cringe-worthy way imaginable.

'Anyone there?'

Angling those linebacker shoulders in their immaculate suit jacket, her visitor called out, then checked behind the counter, around a potted palm, while Roxy bit her lip and wished him gone. She had nothing to say to Nate Sparks and only a limited amount of time to solve the problem surrounding this gown she wore. Make that *problems*—plural. At least three people's futures depended on some answers.

Outside, Nate found some Perfect Dress notepaper on the counter and extracted a thin gold pen from his jacket's inside pocket. Gazing off into the middle distance, he tapped that pen against his strong cleft chin, then, with a swift sure hand, began to write. Roxy poked her nose closer and exquisite Duchess satin rustled against the white-gloss frame.

What could he possibly want to say? *Forgive me for treating you so abysmally. Please come out to dinner.* Not likely. His exit speed would've left a navy torpedo green with envy. Not that he hadn't enjoyed their kiss as much as she had. No one could fake that kind of intensity, even a man who, by all accounts, wasn't short on potential partners. There could be only one explanation for his behaviour that night.

Given they'd met at their respective friends' engagement party and she'd spoken of her profession within the wedding industry in such passionate terms, he must have worried that she'd naturally want to take their amazing first kiss a whole lot further. Like straight down the aisle.

In reality, Roxy believed marriage was an institution not to be taken lightly. Experience said that sustaining a relationship took a whole lot more than the immediate sizzle of emotions and naïve wish for a fairy-tale life. Still, while she might not care to set Nate Sparks straight on her opinion, neither could she hide behind this door for ever. Her sense of dignity, for one, wouldn't allow it.

Shucking back bare shoulders, Roxy filled her lungs, fanned open the door and entered the main room, a long satin stream swishing proudly behind. Nate's attention snapped up and those ice-blue eyes near fell out of his head. Above the knot of his cinnamon-coloured silk tie, his Adam's apple bobbed. A heartbeat later he remembered to smile.

'You're here. I was leaving a note.' His gaze dropped and eyes widened before he pushed out a throaty, nervous laugh. 'Uh, nice outfit. Do you always serve people wearing a wedding gown?'

She couldn't help but bait him.

'Only when I'm feeling lonely.'

When Nate's eyes widened more, Roxy grunted. He didn't know whether to relax and pretend to be a good sport or swap those Pitt Street lace-ups for runners, repeat history and get out while the getting was good. He needn't worry. She'd sooner burn down her shop and play in the ashes than allow him anywhere near her lips again.

Head high, Roxy slipped off her twinkling tiara and set the veil down.

'What can I do for you, Nate?'

'Greg told me this morning. I guess Marla would've told you too.'

She unclipped both diamanté earrings, then weighed them in her palm. After a year-long courtship, 'Their wedding is off.'

The person for whom Roxy had lovingly made this dress was no longer tying the knot. She felt gutted, for Marla's sake mostly but, in truth, also for her own. This gown was the most beautiful she'd ever created...a dress guaranteed to garner interest within industry circles and at a time when she needed it most.

Nate's deep voice lowered more as his gaze intensified. 'Greg's a good friend. My *best* friend.'

'Ditto Marla and me.'

'Dammit, those two belong together.'

'After Marla was slapped in the face by those pictures,' Roxy said, 'she's convinced that they aren't. Frankly, I have to agree with her.'

Roxy's heart flipped over. She knew a little of how Marla had felt. The week after that engagement party incident, Nate's photo had appeared in a gossip magazine. Obviously in his element, he'd been snapped charming a big-breasted woman with swollen lips and hair the colour of rich dark chocolate. Roxy had been so angry—so hurt—she'd torn out the page and ripped it in two.

His jaw tightening, Nate admitted, 'Those photos were incriminating.'

'Her fiancé, intoxicated and handling a near naked woman…' She huffed. 'I don't know what Greg's so-called friend was thinking, publishing those shots on his social media page. And don't you dare say that the "indiscretion" happened at Greg's buck's night. That's no excuse.' Narrowing her eyes, Roxy crossed her arms over her crystal-beaded bodice. 'Where were you anyway? Aren't best men supposed to stop those kinds of things from happening?'

Not that they should ever get anywhere near started.

'I had a meeting early the next morning. I couldn't cancel.'

'I wish things were different—' for more reasons than one '—but Greg did the wrong thing and, frankly, I don't appreciate you showing up here unannounced trying to convince me otherwise.'

She hated seeing Marla so puffy-eyed and bereft. She wished there were some way to help, but listening to a man she already didn't trust, a man who was adept at minimizing bad behaviour—that wasn't the answer. Yes, Greg had always seemed so devoted; however, Roxy knew better than most, sometimes the ones you should be able to rely on were the very ones to watch out for. Given her own past growing up, Roxy supported Marla's decision one hundred per cent. Still, that question remained.

What would become of this gown? She'd held such high hopes for it. For her big designer future.

For months the bridal industry had been abuzz with talk of an incredible opportunity—a contest. The winning gown would take its bow on the Parisian catwalks and feature in *Wedded Bliss*, the world's glossiest wedding publication. Plus, its creator would be awarded a sizable lump sum *and* a year's apprenticeship with New York's leading bridal salon designer.

Roxy had lain awake at night dreaming of claiming the big prize. Since junior high, she'd only ever wanted to design wedding dresses, all kinds of creations to suit all kinds of brides. She couldn't imagine a more exciting or rewarding profession. Five years ago, after completing a number of courses and experience at other shops, she'd set up her own business. But Roxy ached to learn more. *Be* more. All that she could be.

This contest was her chance.

She'd put two hundred per cent into her entry. Last week she'd made the top fifty. She'd bubbled with excitement. For hours had walked on air. But before she could let Marla in on her good news, her friend had broken down and announced that the wedding was off. Since all entries were required to take their big walk down the aisle by the thirty-first of this month, this amazing gown was no

longer eligible for final judging. No wedding equalled
no apprenticeship. No big prize money either. Suddenly
Roxy's recent run of decreased sales and increased bills
seemed all the scarier.

Now, while she set the earrings on their red velvet cush-
ion beneath the counter, deep in thought, Nate paced up
the length of the counter and Roxy's attention drifted to
his hand sliding down the glass surface. It was just a hand,
she told herself. Big. Tanned. Four fingers and a thumb,
five very neat nails. And yet, despite how he'd embarrassed
her that night, she couldn't deny that even now memories of the way he'd held her released a slow wash of tingling warmth deliciously low in her belly. For those few
moments when he'd kissed her so thoroughly, her every
inch had glowed and come alive, a phenomenon that had
left her feeling hot, light and slightly giddy.

A little like she felt now.

Damn the man!

Her cheeks burning, Roxy siphoned down a breath,
gathered herself and caught the last of Nate's comment.

'...must be something we can do to get them back
together.'

Closing the counter drawer, she refocused on her
friend's situation as well as her own. Lifting her chin,
Roxy made herself clear.

'Whatever you have in mind, count me *out*.'

As Nate held Roxanne Trammel's determined gaze he
knotted his arms securely over his chest.

Of medium height. Nothing bombshell about the body.
Voice on the soft rather than smoky side. Her gestures
weren't exceptional. Neither were her walk or her laugh.
And yet *something* about this woman was incontestably,
frustratingly alluring.

Nate accepted that reality same way he accepted that

steel softened at a predetermined temperature. A similar temperature to the one his blood had reached when he'd given himself over to Roxy's lure six months ago. He'd hated leaving her looking so confused and pained that night, but he'd also vowed that their first kiss would be their last: should they happen to come within each other's orbit again—at a mutual friends' wedding, for example—he would not permit a repeat performance, no matter if the continuation of the human race depended on it.

That outfit she wore now ought to be reminder and turn-off enough. He was a self-determining man, a bachelor who intended to stay that way. And yet looking into those thickly lashed, sparkling green eyes now, he had to concentrate to keep from reaching out and making mammoth mistake number two. Only this time—if he caved and brought her crushingly close again—he wasn't certain he would stop.

Crossing to the end of the counter, she said, 'I don't know why you're stepping up now to defend him. Greg's responsible for his own actions, even if he obviously needs a watcher.' She shrugged. 'Hope your meeting was worth it.'

'Depends if you count a huge opportunity for launching a business venture that both Greg and I had worked on for months worth it.'

'You're becoming partners? From what Marla's told me, Greg's committed to the family business.'

Nate held that breath. He didn't want to lay bare any secrets. But he did need her help to get those two reunited, which meant coughing up some answers and rebuilding a little good faith here. So, when Roxy in all her finery moved to lift a small cardboard box from the floor, he stepped up to help at the same time he replied.

'Greg's wanted to break out on his own for a while.'

He took the box from her arms and set it on the counter, after which Roxy opened the lid and extracted a frilly mauve garter. Nate's gaze zeroed in on the lace and words came to mind. Seductive. *Sexy*. Guess a bridal salon sold all kinds of accessories.

Mulling, Roxy ran the silk loop around her index fingers once, twice. 'His family owns a big steel company, right?'

'PrimeSteel. A manufacturer and distributor of steel and finished steel products. I work in management for a rival company.'

As he spoke she opened a nearby drawer and, peering through the counter's glass ceiling, arranged the garter on its own rumpled satin bed.

'Greg and I met through industry contacts,' he went on, his voice a little deeper than before. 'We shared similar views about the future of steel, more specifically, colour-bonded products. Given the economy and environmental issues, we think the opportunities in *less expensive* and *environmentally effective* are endless.'

He expected to hear back regarding the most relevant patent application soon, then they could truly move forward.

'So you joined forces?' Roxy asked.

When she moved to extract another goodie from that box—a gossamer-thin, ultra-short negligee—Nate blinked and, in a heartbeat, imagined her wearing it. He saw the swell of her cleavage, a taut midriff too. He knew her skin would be smooth and warm, just as the sweep of her lips had been that night.

With a start, Nate blinked again...brought himself back. While Roxy arranged the negligee beside that garter, he cleared his throat and, diverting his focus, brushed down then inspected the tail of his tie.

'Greg and I decided that we needed a big investor to do this and do it right. Last week, a prospective investor landed in Sydney. On the phone, Bob Nichols liked our business model, was interested in hearing more but, having hundreds of balls to juggle while he was here, he was short on time. Before heading back to Texas, he made himself available at five a.m. last Sunday—the morning after Greg's buck's party.'

'How does Greg's father feel about his son leaving the family business?'

'Mr Martin's not happy. He's supportive of Greg but in exchange for that support he expects total loyalty, to the family, to the company.'

Returning to the box, she extracted a white satin triangle no larger than a skewed playing card. With its thin elasticized straps dangling from her fingers, she moved to lay that piece beneath the counter too—alongside that garter and X-rated slip.

As her hand smoothed over the display Nate's pulse quickened and beat in his ears because now he imagined Roxy standing in a dimly lit room wearing it all—garter, nightie, that provocative scrap of a thong. In his mind, while he lowered to kneel before her and shaped his palms over her hips, she sighed out his name, filed her fingers through his hair and, stepping closer, brought his head near.

From far away, he heard her ask, 'So, was your Mr Nichols still interested after your meeting?'

The real world faded back.

'Absolutely. Not that it matters. Greg and I spoke this morning. Since Marla called the wedding off, he's lost all motivation. For the time being Greg's staying on at PrimeSteel.'

'Why not go ahead on your own? With Mr Nichols, I mean.'

Her tone added, *And leave me alone.*

'This was *our* project and I know Greg will be sorry if he pulls out now.'

She cocked a brow. 'And?'

He exhaled and gave it up. 'And two heads with steel manufacturing knowledge are better than one.'

He was comfortable with his abilities but in business—in life—a person needed as much reinforcement as possible. It was a slippery slope into failure and obscurity. His own father's descent into near poverty had taught Nate that lesson well.

Roxy dipped a hand back into that box. Before she could pull out God knew what, Nate swiped that box of goodies off the counter and set it safely on the floor.

'I think,' he said, 'if we get Greg and Marla alone, she'll hear his side of the story and accept that those pictures painted him in an unfair light.'

'Oh, gee, you think?'

Studying her mock pitying look, knowing there was something more behind it, he said, 'They'll work this out.'

'Then they'll keep their date at the church,' she surmised, 'and you'll get your business partner back.'

Correct. 'Question is—are you on board?'

'You must be hard of hearing. I already said count me out.'

'Give me some time and I'll convince you.'

Her too-kissable mouth tightened.

'No.'

He growled, cursing under his breath. 'Five lousy minutes. I have a plan. It could mean the difference between your friend's ultimate happiness and a lifetime of loneliness.'

'So dramatic.'

He frowned. 'Yeah, well, it's pretty damn important to them.'

'And Mr Goodie-two-shoes you has nothing at stake.'

This time he bit back the growl and pierced her with a judgmental glare.

'This isn't about Greg and his buck's party, is it? It's not about whether you want to help stop your friend from making perhaps the biggest mistake of her life. You're being obstinate and surly now because of what happened between us all those months ago. You felt jilted and you're prepared to let your friend suffer because you have a beef with me.'

Her eyes rounded with affront and anger. 'If you think that argument will help your cause, you have more ego than even I gave you credit for. Ever hear the saying, water finds its own level? You treat women like chattels. Chances are you choose friends of a similar nature. But neither of you like being called out for it.'

Words burned on the tip of his tongue, but he wouldn't give her the satisfaction of acting the way she anticipated and cutting her down. He was ready to tell her to forget he'd even suggested she help, forget he was ever here.

In fact, she could go to hell.

He strode for the exit, swung back the door and barely refrained from slamming it shut behind him. He was half-way down the busy city block, near colliding with oblivious passers-by, when the steam clouding his brain cooled a degree and his locomotive pace slowed down. As much as he was attracted to Roxanne Trammel, she was a giant thorn in his side. He'd be wise never to see her again, under any circumstances.

But, if he were truthful, he understood her upset over

his departure that night. He'd never done such a thing before and apologizing as he'd hightailed it away didn't rub off any of the tarnish. But Roxy didn't want a confession. She did, however, want to help her friend. He was convinced that Marla should at least hear Greg out, and that wouldn't happen unless he swallowed his pride, turned around and tried to persuade Roxy one more time.

Roxy was still standing at the counter in that wedding gown, staring blindly at the accessories under that glass counter, when the doorbell tinkled and, hat in hand, he edged inside the shop again. She looked over and, straightening, opened her mouth. But he held up a hand.

'Before you run me out of town again, let me say I was a jerk for bringing up that other night. It won't happen again. But I can't walk away without asking you one more time to help give those two the chance they deserve, the chance Marla would want if she were thinking clearly.'

'Maybe she *is* thinking clearly.'

Weary now, he exhaled. Her middle name was stubborn. 'Just give me five minutes to tell you what I have in mind.'

She tilted her head, thought some more.

'Five minutes?' she finally said. 'That's it?'

'Won't even take that long.'

She almost grinned. 'Anyone would think you were sure of yourself.'

'About this, I am.'

She set her hands on her satin-clad hips. After another tense moment, she visibly relaxed and inspected her dress.

'Let me change first.' Her lips twitched. 'I don't want to give you hives.'

Moving through that back door again, she lobbed a final remark over her shoulder. 'If someone happens to walk in looking for their perfect dress, tell them I'll be right out.'

But it was well after five on a Friday—closing time. 'Why don't I just flip the sign over?'

'Don't you dare.' He barely caught her last words as she disappeared out back. 'I need every sale I can get.'

People in business had to be aggressive, but the energy behind that last remark was one hell of an admission. The way she'd spoken six months ago, Roxy lived for the thrill of owning this shop—for the privilege of personally contributing to the 'magic of marriage'—but it sounded as if her enterprise wasn't doing so well. Would she want to go ahead with helping Greg and Marla when she knew his plan? That she'd need to leave her shop unattended or alternatively manned for a few days? Perhaps if the deal included watching him being hung, drawn and quartered…

Admittedly, his behaviour that night had been less than chivalrous, but God knew he'd had his reasons for leaving, just as Roxy had had hers for latching on the way she had. Clearly she was in the market for a serious partner of her own. What was so wrong with letting her know he wasn't up for grabs? Surely that was better than leading her on.

The bell above the door rang and two women edged inside; from the age difference and resemblance, Nate suspected mother and daughter. He strolled over to a rack of dresses and feigned interest. Roxy might be difficult, she might play havoc with his equilibrium, but, even if her shop were raking in millions, he wouldn't get in the way of a possible sale. People liked space. He imagined that went double for brides searching for a wedding dress.

So he thumbed through some size six to tens while going over the points of his plan for Marla and Greg yet again. Aside from needing to vacate Sydney for a few days, he wondered whether Roxy would entertain the idea of taking on such an active role or even if Greg and Marla would fall for it. Marla would then need to get past the mistrust and hurt those pictures had caused.

On the other side of the room, the women were involved in a hushed conversation. Eavesdropping wasn't Nate's style; however, the words he caught worried him enough to push scruples aside.

'We won't find anything,' the daughter bemoaned. 'It's suburbia. You saw the sign. My God, she sews them herself.'

'We're here, Violet,' the mother encouraged. 'Let's look a while. You never know what you'll find.'

Coat hangers clicked down a steel rod. Satin and silk rustled, and Violet sighed. 'No. No. No. No.' A second, more impatient sigh. 'A waste of time.'

Nate hadn't a clue; women's fashion wasn't his forte. But ignorance and prejudging were two different beasts. Clearly Violet had made up her mind before entering the store. If she took off her blinkers, bet she'd find something worth another look. Perhaps even worth buying.

Roxy had said she needed every sale. Given she was at least prepared to listen to his plan, why not return the favour and see if he couldn't help here?

With a dress in hand, he rotated around and, as impatient as that woman's sighs had been, his was filled with satisfaction.

'This is perfect. My God, she'll love it.' His smile big, Nate nodded a greeting then apologised to the ladies. 'Sorry. Thinking aloud.'

Curious, Violet looked around. 'Is your fiancée in a dressing room?'

'I asked her to meet me here. I can't wait till she sees this dress.'

One of the mother's pencilled eyebrows lifted. 'I've never heard of a groom choosing his bride's gown.'

'Emma's been everywhere, including interstate. She was thinking of having one made and a friend recommended this place. She was so disheartened. She'd even talked about calling the whole thing off.'

The daughter gasped. *'No.'*

'She's the woman of my dreams,' he said. 'I want to have babies with Emma. Lots of them.'

Now Violet and her mother's eyes were shining with approval, so Nate hammed it up. He hadn't been given his senior production's lead in *Ali Baba* for nothing.

'I never thought I could love someone like I love my Emma. I just need to help her find that perfect dress.'

'That's what this place is called,' Violet whispered in her mother's ear loud enough for Nate to hear. 'The Perfect Dress.'

'It is a pretty gown,' the mother agreed, taking more notice of Nate's impromptu choice.

'Don't ask me how I know but I do.' With an enamoured air, he shrugged. 'My Emma will look like an angel in this.'

Having moved to another rack, Mother drew out a gown.

'Sweetheart,' she called. 'Look. This beading is exquisite. Did you say the owner sews these all herself?'

Violet examined the dress, draped it close. When she began to sway back and forth, searching for a mirror, Nate intervened again. A sign hung over the entrance to a nearby corridor.

'The change rooms are that way,' he said with a slant of his head.

But now Violet had found the price tag and told her mother, 'I know you said not to worry about cost, but…' When Violet mouthed the amount, Nate overheard and near fell over. Did women honestly spend that much on a single dress?

Fortunately, Mother didn't bat an eyelid. She dashed away Violet's concerns with a wave of her diamond-clad hand and both women had trundled off when Nate's ears pricked at a persistent *pssst*. He pivoted around.

Hiding behind that door, Roxy was madly waving him over. Nate hung up the dress and crossed the room—not fast enough, it seemed. Her hand shot out and hauled him inside.

'What are you doing?'

Gathering himself as she shut the door, he lengthened his neck and straightened his tie. 'Drumming up business.'

She looked as if he'd admitted to eating chocolate-covered tarantulas for lunch.

'You can't lie like that.'

'It's not lying.' The way he saw it, 'I'm creating an opportunity.'

Horrified, she leaned back against the door. 'I hate to think of the opportunity you've concocted for Marla and Greg.' Gathering herself, she pulled up tall. 'You can't come waltzing in here and making up stories. This is my place of business. I depend on my reputation.'

'How did I harm your good name?'

'If those two ever find out and take it further, the legal term I think is *fraud*.'

'They'll never find out.'

She held the bridge of her nose. 'Maybe I should go out and just come clean.'

Outside, the desk bell pinged. Roxy jumped, called out, 'I'll be right there,' then glanced down at the gown she still wore.

Which, frankly, looked great on her. The white satin suited her skin's natural glow. The sweep of her waist in that bodice was hypnotic.

Not that he would allow himself to be concerned with

any of that. He was here to get his plan on the table and any bugs ironed out before they went ahead with Operation Back Together.

He said, 'I thought you were changing.'

'I couldn't get a hold of the zip.' She whirled around. As the train slapped his shin, he was presented with a tantalizing rear view. 'You'll have to help.'

Alarm bells—red and flashing—went off in his head. An invitation and bare flesh equalled temptation. Sure, what Roxy proposed seemed innocent enough but, in essence, she was asking him to help her undress. To open himself up and be vulnerable to the call of his baser urges, which he had trouble enough containing where Roxy Trammel was concerned.

He held up his palms. 'I'll pass.'

'You can't *pass*.'

Believe me, 'It's safer I don't.'

'I trust you not to do any damage.' When he didn't budge, she groaned and muttered, 'Okay. Time to get this out in the open.' Her fists finding her hips, she rotated again. 'I won't lie and say I didn't enjoy the kiss we shared that night because, while I'm loath to admit it, I did. And I admit my reaction was…enthusiastic. But if you think I'm so desperate that I'd use sex to manipulate a marriage proposal, think again. And if I *were* to do such an abhorrent thing—' her nose rose a regal notch '—it wouldn't be with you.' She hesitated, then went on. 'In fact, I've been kissed since and, frankly, yours pales in comparison.'

Nate's gape turned into a smirk. And she called *him* a liar. He knew just how much she'd enjoyed that kiss. Almost as much as he had.

Still, if she could play this Arctic ice-shelf cool, couldn't he? Hell, it was only a zip. She wasn't asking him to slip

off a garter or nightdress or that itty-bitty pair of silk pant-
ies—which he'd best not think about right now.

When he lifted his chin, she lifted hers. He twirled
his finger—*turn around*—and, hoisting up her skirt, she
whirled again.

The dress's back was scooped low and, with her long
fair hair twisted up, Nate was greeted by an unobstructed,
blemish-free landscape. Delicate twin shoulder blades
bracketed a sweep of smooth tan skin and two accidental
curls spiralled either side of the dent of her spine.

Pleasant warmth pooled then solidified high on Nate's
thighs. But he took a deep breath and, focusing not on the
view but the task, doggedly searched. After a full-on few
seconds, he huffed. No wonder she couldn't find it.

'There *is* no zip.'

'It's invisible,' she told him. 'Feel around inside the
bodice facing.'

Nate scratched his head. Did she say invisible? And,
'Bodice *what*?'

'Slide your finger up and down the inside top of the
seam.' She dropped a wry look over one shoulder. 'You
do know what a seam is, don't you?'

'A rich deposit where minerals are found.'

She rolled her eyes as if to say, *Men*. 'Just don't tug
too hard.'

When she turned back, Nate shook out his hands,
rubbed his palms together. Not sweaty. Not cold. All good.
He edged one fingertip inside.

Her skin was toasty-warm and smooth as the satin. And
now he was aware that she was wearing the same perfume she had that fateful night. Subtle. Something with
lavender? Whatever the ingredients, the scent was light
and fresh and...

Nate filled his lungs.

The kind of bouquet I could breathe in all day.

He snapped open eyes that seemed to have drifted shut.

Roxy had implied that she'd dated since their evening together. Leaning closer, he slid his thumb down and felt around. He hated himself for needing to ask but couldn't a guy be curious?

'So, I take it you're seeing someone.'

'No one in particular.'

Chewing that over, he found something small and difficult to grab high at the top of the crease. Squeezing just enough to get a grip, he added, 'And yet *someone's* swept you off your feet.'

Those curls tickled the back of his hand as she purred. 'I've been swept off several times since that night.'

His bite tightened and grip firmed more. He was jiggling in earnest when, outside, the desk bell rang again.

'I'll be right out,' Roxy called pleasantly, then to him, 'What's taking so long?'

'Inexperience,' he growled. With a wedding gown, at least. This darn thing didn't glide as it should.

'Don't force it,' she told him.

'I'm not forcing anything.'

Shifting, he began to work it in a hopefully more fruitful and earnest kind of way. Clearly this exercise needed a little more of the ol' Nate Sparks finesse.

Three seconds later, she complained, 'You're too rough.'

'Relax.' His fingertips rolled, then tugged and rolled again. 'Just a few seconds more.'

'Nate, not so hard.'

'Almost got it—'

The zip suddenly gave.

Actually what gave was the fabric splitting either side.

While Roxy stiffened, Nate's heart stopped beating as he held his breath and stared.

It wasn't much of a tear. Really barely noticeable. But when Roxy turned around, her expression said it all. Her face was a mask of disbelief, anguish. *Rage.* And her eyes, which had looked merely annoyed earlier, now spat green fire.

'Tell me you didn't tear the dress,' she groaned. 'You didn't, did you? Not *this* dress.'

The anger in her eyes turned to fear then they edged with moisture and Nate felt the walls press in.

'It's not too bad.' He indicated with his fingers. 'Maybe an inch.' Maximum two.

That call from outside came again.

'Anyone there?'

'Coming,' Roxy said, but this time her voice cracked.

What could he say? If he could take it back, he would. 'Roxy…'

Her eyes filling, she inhaled and in a heartbeat all her angst and energy seemed to drain away. She pressed her lips together. Swallowed. Shrugged.

'Doesn't matter anyway,' she muttered and he frowned.

'*What* doesn't matter?' When she swished out of the room, he followed. 'Roxy, answer me.'

'It doesn't matter,' she replied, 'because this gown is— or was—Marla's.'

Nate gaped. He'd wrecked his mate's fiancée's gown? Not a good omen. And why was the bride's best friend wearing it anyway?

When he joined Roxy out front, she was looking around an empty room. Seemed those potential customers had given up and gone home. But then that same enquiring voice rang out again, this time from the direction of the dressing rooms. A moment later, that older woman appeared. On seeing them, she clasped her cheeks with glee.

'Oh, my. This must be your beautiful bride-to-be. And

you're right,' the woman went on before speaking directly to Roxy rather than Nate. 'That gown suits you to a T. My Violet thinks she might have found the right one too.'

'Really? That's wonderful.' Roxy's disappointment at that accidental rip transformed into a frail but hope-filled smile. Then she evaluated her own gown. 'But this dress…' Her cheeks pinked up and she rubbed her brow. 'Well, it's a little hard to explain.'

The woman angled in. 'No need. My Violet went through the same thing,' she confided. 'Anxiety. So many decisions.' Her shoulders squared. 'But when you've found a man who's so obviously in love with you, so committed, how can things not fall into place? You're a lucky woman.' She slid that smile Nate's way. 'A lucky couple.'

Nate smothered a wince. The woman had it wrong. Roxy wasn't Emma. There *was* no Emma and wouldn't be for a very long while, if he could help it.

The woman looked between the uncertain two, then slanted her head. 'Is there something wrong with the gown, dear?'

'Oh, no,' Roxy said. 'I *love* it. More than any gown ever. The satin's as soft as rose petals. Every line is exquisite. It's just that this dress is—'

'Beautiful,' Nate cut in when he knew he ought to have let her finish and set the misunderstanding straight. But the dress *was* stunning, he thought again, drinking in those satiny curves and falls, whether Marla ended up wearing it or not.

When Roxy's slow smile said she appreciated his compliment, a kernel of heat bloomed in his chest, a sensation he enjoyed as much as he spurned. Then she turned and admitted to the woman, 'But I'm not this man's fiancée.'

The woman blinked. 'I don't understand.'

'I own this salon. I'm Roxanne Trammel.'

The woman absorbed the news and, nodding absently, introduced herself as Ava Morris before her focus swung to Nate. 'Where's your bride-to-be? Nothing's wrong, I hope.'

Nate scrubbed his jaw. He'd only meant to help—to give Roxy a hand up with a potential sale. But duplicity, well intended or not, had caught up. Nothing for it but to face the music.

'Actually,' he began, 'my fiancée's—'

'Out back,' Roxy said, cutting in. 'Emma's choosing accessories.'

Mrs Morris held her stomach and breathed out over a relieved smile. 'Well, that was quick!'

'Happens like that sometimes,' Roxy said, slipping Nate a 'you owe me' look.

A call from the dressing room. *'Can someone help with this?'*

Picking up her skirts, Roxy went to hurry off but Mrs Morris put up a hand.

'I'll help Violet. You see to your other matter.'

Mrs Morris rushed away while, sheepish, Nate tugged his ear. 'Sorry about the Emma thing.'

'You shouldn't have lied. I in no way condone it.' Roxy's expression lightened a smidge. 'But I do appreciate you trying to help. I didn't need to embarrass you.'

As he'd embarrassed her that night?

But she didn't look half as ticked off as she had a moment ago. In fact, her eyes were almost smiling, somehow reaching out. And he liked the positive change. Liked it way too much.

Nate cleared his throat and hauled himself back. 'We'll need to see each other again. To discuss the Marla-Greg plan,' he clarified quickly.

'I'll give you my email address.' She cut across the counter and slipped a business card from a holder. 'Why don't you send over your ideas for Greg and Marla? I'll be with Violet for a while yet hopefully.'

'I'd rather toss around ideas face to face.'

'I don't know what time I'll be free.'

'I could hang around. Help out some more. Maybe do some zip repairs.' His weak smile faded and he tucked in his chin. 'I really am sorry about that.'

She tried to hold her scowl. 'Guess you can't help if you're too strong for your own good.'

'I should have taken more time.' Thought ahead.

Hell, maybe he shouldn't have come at all. But he believed in Greg and couldn't abandon him. He believed in their business too, and he definitely wouldn't abandon that. There seemed no other way around this bind, and to pull this make-up plan off he needed help. He needed Roxy.

Looking radiant beneath the lights, she offered over the card, but Nate found his attention drawn instead to the side of her throat where a tiny pulse popped. Strange, but at this moment he seemed to feel that heartbeat as well as he felt his own. Steady. Deep.

Hot.

When she tipped closer, still offering the card, Nate extended a hand and accepted. He hadn't meant for his fingers to linger, to stretch that bit further and brush over hers. And in that instant he saw the pulse in her throat beat faster and her gaze grow heavy while his dropped to her glossy parted lips.

Time and again, he'd wondered what would've happened if he'd stayed that night six months ago. What principle of physics decreed that he would share his father's fate, as well as his grandfather's, and back on down the line? But as he continued to drink in Roxy's curious gaze the world fell away and a series of snapshots flashed through his mind…

His parents on their wedding day, two months after
they'd met. His grandfather and grandmother in tails and
lacy veil six weeks on the heels of a first date. If ever he
mentioned the myth, his father would simply shrug. When
a Sparks man found the right woman—the one who left
his senses reeling and blood crashing like giant rollers on
a shore—nothing else mattered. He might as well surrender. The toll of wedding bells was imminent. Marriage
and domesticity a foregone. So, it would seem, was lack
of personal growth and motivation for building security
for one's future.

After marrying, his father had given up his dream of
finishing medical school and becoming a surgeon. Instead
he'd taken a job as a hospital wardsman, which meant less
income to support the five kids that came along but more
time to spend with his beloved wife, the only thing in his
life that seemed to matter. Not always as romantic as it
might sound.

Nate couldn't forget the weeks his mother had spent
convalescing after a car accident when he was twelve. The
children had needed leadership, strength, hope. Instead,
their father had stopped eating, stopped communicating.
He'd all but pined away for love. Or the time his father had
had the chance to return to his education but had decided to
support his wife's dream of becoming a renowned painter
when, hell, they could barely afford to feed themselves, let
alone buy art materials and exhibition space.

Similar stories of Sparks men and their women had sur-
vived…hasty marriages followed by a lifetime of Byronic
devotion. Was it genetics or a curse? Of course it could
all be coincidence.

It was only when Nate realized his other palm had
curled around the satin cinching her waist—when Roxy

trembled and his head dropped deliberately over hers—
that he knew the truth.

Coincidence had nothing to do with it.

He should have run while he could.

CHAPTER TWO

WHEN his throat made a gravelled wanting sound that resonated like beautiful bass chords through Roxy's bones, memories of the dreams that had tormented her these past months wrapped around her like a run of steamy veils. A heartbeat later, his mouth captured hers and inhibitions concerning Nate Sparks and his dubious affections spread their powerful wings and flew far away.

In the smoky recesses of her mind she understood she'd submitted without a whimper of protest. More so, she was aware of her breasts, suddenly so full and sensitive, rubbing against the front of his business shirt...against the hard broad plateau of his chest. After all her talk, after the way he'd escaped that night, she ought to be ashamed by her surrender now. She should be *horrified*.

She was anything but.

The magic of his kiss was still as strong. In fact, the pleasure he stirred up within her had only grown. The verdict was back, approved, stamped and sealed. Their lips were a perfect fit, and the desire pulsing through her veins was a better than fair indicator that their bodies would join just as well.

She focused on individual sensations but absorbed them all at once...the graze of his jaw, the drugging pull of his scent, the mesmerizing way he seemed to *consume* her.

The sensations were so pure, it was nothing short of sweet torture. Then his palms ironed up and over the curve of her back, pressing her that much closer, and Roxy dissolved even more.

No man could compete with the depth of longing Nate Sparks had brought out in her. Ridiculous as it might seem, she was helpless to deny it. She wanted him to make love to her—*take* her. After one craze-filled moment, she wanted that so completely, she couldn't remember a time when anything had mattered more.

Of course, something did.

His kiss shifted then lightened so that rather than covering, his mouth was now brushing hers. On a dreamy smile, she held his bristled jaw and murmured, soft and sexy against the bow of his lower lip, *'Gotcha.'*

Nate stiffened. His eyes flew open, enlarged pupils shrank, then he jumped back as if someone had rammed his stomach with a stick. His lips pressed together while he drove a hand over his scalp, leaving usually neatly groomed hair nicely dishevelled.

Roxy's smile widened.

Damn, it felt good to be right.

'What the hell are you doing?' he rasped.

Satisfied, she slapped her hands as if removing grit. 'Proving something.'

'Proving *what*?'

'That the world didn't end.'

Nate's face thundered and his jaw clenched doubly tight.

But then the fury and shock cleared, the tension locking his stance visibly eased and his eyes took on the gleam of a wry smile. All in all, he looked rather pleased with himself.

'You *are* right,' he said. 'The world didn't end. The sky wasn't ripped open by a thousand raging thunderbolts.

There's nothing wrong with physical reaction to stimulation. Sexual arousal happens every day.'

And *that* was why he'd run that night six months ago. Why he was acting overly cavalier now. Which was fine by her. She had enough going wrong with her life without inviting in more trouble.

'Hope you don't take offence,' she said in a flat tone, 'but I need to follow up on Ava and Violet.'

Giving a curt nod, he dug out a business card of his own. 'Ring when you're finished here.'

'That could be late.'

He flashed a thin grin. 'I'm a night owl.'

After slapping the card on the counter, he strode out and the invisible band squeezing her windpipe eased.

She'd daydreamed of how she might one day turn the tables and make Nate feel as small as she had that night when he'd left her quaking and embarrassed as she'd never been before. Seeing his reaction now had been worth the price of stirring up all those wonderful, dreadful feelings again. Primal emotions that demanded immediate attention but needed to be shut down and ignored.

Still...

Remembering, Roxy touched her tingling lips.

No one kissed like Nate Sparks.

'Hey, buddy, great game.'

Rounding up a squash match at Greg Martin's private home court, Nate clapped his friend on the back as they moved into a change room that boasted three showers, a sauna and facilities for remedial massage. Nate hadn't mentioned Marla and their bust-up yet but he planned to. He was committed to helping mend Greg's fractured life—both personal and professional—even at the risk of exposing himself to public enemy number one. The girl with the lips.

Shaking off the residual effects of his and Roxy's latest bombshell kiss, Nate grabbed a towel while Greg dropped his racket on the bench. The clatter echoed around the ceiling and walls.

'I played like a dog,' Greg said before dragging his shirt up and over a crop of sandy-coloured hair. 'But I appreciate the company. The alternative was dinner with the folks. Don't think I could stand my mother's questions tonight, or my father turning red, trying to contain his relief.'

Happy that his son was staying with the family firm, Nate surmised, stuffing his racket into his bag.

'We're going to sort this out. You didn't hire that stripper on your buck's night, you didn't call her over to sit on your lap and you certainly didn't ask for those shots to be snapped in the brief window of time she was there. Woody Cox did all that.' One of Greg's buddies since university. Nate had always thought that guy needed a leash. 'Hell, he even admitted to putting the evidence on the Net.'

'He apologised as soon as I balled him out.'

'Not soon enough.' News on social media networks spread quicker than a wink. Sometimes a great thing. In this case, just plain dumb. 'But Marla can't stay mad for ever.'

'You think? A few words on the phone—her crying, me begging—and she refuses to see me again, let alone marry me.' Greg's towel swiped down his unshaven face, around the thick column of his neck. 'I've sent a truck full of flowers, a diamond bracelet to go with the ring. I even hired a scaffold and played a slideshow of all our best moments outside of her second-storey window. She pitched our framed engagement photo at the screen. Tore a two-foot rip down the middle.'

Nate forced a Pollyanna smile. 'After getting that out of her system, she might be ready to talk.'

'When she emailed our guest list and said the wedding was off, what could I do?'

Seriously? 'Not *give up*.'

There was a reason he and Greg were friends. They thought the same. Shared similar values. Nate knew Greg would never cheat on a woman because Nate, himself, would never do such a thing. Not that he was naïve enough to think indiscretions between couples didn't happen.

At the engagement party six months ago, he and Roxy had been talking out on the restaurant's balcony when she'd mentioned her father and his exploits. She hadn't belaboured the point but had rather only said enough to make her situation growing up clear. Life was confusing for a kid when your dad was a womanizer and your mother refused to see the situation for what it was: a betrayal not only to wife but also to child.

Guess there were some advantages to that blasted family curse, Nate thought as he drew the sweat-damp shirt off over his head. Despite the downsides, he was thankful his parents' marriage was a solid one. They didn't argue over anything more important than where to spend their next vacation. If their trust should ever be tested, neither would look at the other with suspicion. Not that his dad would ever come close to cheating. And neither would Greg.

His friend was jamming his shirt into his bag, muttering, 'Hell, maybe Marla's better off without me.'

'Like Sparks Martin Steel would be better off without you?'

Greg's dark gaze edged over. 'I know you're disappointed but, believe me, it's best you go that alone. I'm no good to anyone right now. I'd only let you down.' He headed for the exit, his six-plus height barely missing the lintel. 'I'm going to take a shower inside.'

Nate punched his arms through the sleeves of a fresh shirt, then followed Greg out. Time to set down the first layer of his plan.

'Why don't you and I get away for a couple of days? You had time pencilled out anyway.'

Time off to finalize wedding stuff with Marla.

'I'd be sorry company.' Outside in the evening cool and beneath path lights, Greg turned and sent a wan smile. 'I'm beat. I'll catch you later in the week.'

As Greg made his way down the path that led to his separate quarters on his parents' extravagant Potts Point estate, Nate set his jaw. Dammit, he wasn't giving up on that wedding. He certainly wasn't giving up on his and Greg's partnership. This was only the first round and, no matter the setbacks or complications, he was in for the long haul.

When his cell vibrated and buzzed in his sports bag, Nate checked the ID and his heartbeat began to crash. Speaking of complications...

Shoring himself, Nate connected and Roxy Trammel purred down the line.

'Is that Luscious Lips?'

'That's not funny.' Neither the nickname nor her tone. He'd done the wrong thing that night, but couldn't she show him a little mercy six months on? He'd fallen hook, line and sinker when she'd given herself over to their embrace. Now her voice was tease enough.

If history was anything to go by, it wouldn't take too many more embraces like the one this afternoon to have him looking cross-eyed, thinking he was in love and arranging a whole new set of priorities. The mere thought of the way her body had moved against his could make him break into a sweat that had nothing to do with the energetic hour he'd just spent on the court. If it killed him—and it probably near would—from now on he'd keep his hands to himself.

'Are we still on for tonight?' she asked.

Regarding Marla and Greg? 'You bet. Have you eaten?'

'I have a craving for sushi.'

Sauntering to his car, Nate winced. 'Raw dead fish.'

'Who knew you were so cultured?'

'I vote Chinese.'

'Done.' She suggested a well-known restaurant.

'Say, thirty minutes? I need to change.'

'Just for you, I'll change too. All this white satin is getting heavy.'

He heard her laugh before signing off and, despite his mood, Nate couldn't help himself. He laughed too.

Roxy arrived at the China Town restaurant bang on time.

The expansive room was bordered by tall arched windows, smelled of fine Asian cuisine and was illuminated by a sky of glowing pumpkin-shaped lanterns. A slender woman dressed in a red full-length cheongsam led her to a table and when Roxy pulled in her chair, she knew Nate would appreciate their location: dead centre of the restaurant, in plain view of everyone. That second kiss had been even more unsettling than the first; neither she nor Nate needed to be tested by sharing a darkened corner tonight. Her outfit had also been chosen with those same boundaries in mind.

A 'tailored black trousers, loose-fitting black silk shirt with matching casual vest' combo was more 'business' than 'come hither'. Spiked sandal heels were a staple with this outfit but tonight it was boots. No sheer silk stockings either. Thick, black, to the breastbone tights, as well as her ugliest bra. Who could get turned on wearing old stretched cotton? Amazing what a person found stuffed at the back of their lingerie drawer.

Roxy glanced across at the entrance—no Nate—so she filled her water glass from a centre pitcher then inspected the table setting. Skimming a fingertip over the symbols printed on her Chinese zodiac placemat, she smiled. The years indicated she was a tiger! Powerful, passionate.

Reading on, she frowned.

Restless, *reckless*? What sign would Nate fall under? An agile rabbit might fit. Or an arrogant monkey. She huffed and flicked out her napkin.

Bet he was a loner snake, waiting for some unsuspecting victim to mesmerize.

When he strode in five minutes later, looking drop-dead amazing in chinos and casual button-down, Roxy skulled her ice-water to keep her over-heated imagination from going up in flames. So much for the power of pathetic underwear.

His dark hair was post-shower damp and his shoulders tonight appeared even broader. He'd forgone a shave and the bristled shadow smudging his strong square jaw only served to make his presence all the more entrancing. Knowing he was near, she felt tingles race over her skin, brushing her most sensitive spots and making them glow.

Could a man grow sexier in a matter of hours?

He caught sight of her and crossed over with a fluid strong gait that had every woman in the room blindly setting down chopsticks and turning her head. At the table, he beckoned a passing waiter at the same time he dragged in his chair.

'I'll need something a little stronger,' he said as she refilled her water glass. 'Care to share a bottle of red?'

'No alcohol for me.'

'Need to keep your wits about you?'

She blinked at the tease glittering in his lidded blue eyes. But after her 'luscious lips' comment earlier, she'd allow him one ace. Frankly, she didn't need her inhibitions weakened tonight. Not that she would admit that now.

'I have to be in the shop early,' she said. 'Busy week coming up.'

'Actually, I wanted to talk to you about that.'

Before he could explain, that waiter arrived and Nate ordered a glass of Cabernet Sauvignon.

'To have any hope of enticing Greg and Marla back together,' he said as the waiter moved off, 'you need to speak with your friend about getting away from Sydney for a few days. Somewhere isolated where she can't jump on the next plane out and escape before really hearing him through.'

'Sorry.' Shutting one eye, Roxy turned her head slightly. 'Think I'm having auditory hallucinations.'

He spoke up. 'We'll need to send Greg there too, of course.'

'Without either of them knowing?' Roxy fought the urge to laugh. This was his plan? 'Are you crazy? A, they'll hate you for ever for tricking them. B, short of leading them by the nose, they'll never go.'

'Precisely. I'll take Greg. You take Marla.'

'You want me to take Marla out to some isolated destination so she can meet with Greg and verbally tear his head off again?'

'I want to see them together so they can work through this. We'll keep them on track.'

'We. As in you and me? You expect me to leave Sydney, my shop, to go trekking off to God only knows where with *you*?' Astonished, she sat back. 'I have a business to run.'

'Put someone else on at the shop.'

Roxy wanted to get up and leave, then and there. He really was an arrogant son of a...

Dragging down a calming breath, she put her thoughts back on track.

After Violet's deposit this afternoon, the books were almost square. When the minor alterations were done and the dress delivered, the balance would put her business back in the black. That didn't mean she could afford to slack off. The economy was dead. People cut corners, even on must-haves like a perfect wedding dress. She had to keep her eye on the bottom line.

'If you need some funds,' he said, as if reading her thoughts, 'to see your way through, I can help.'

'You really are mad if you think I'd accept anything from you.'

'You're being obstinate.'

She exploded. 'You don't *get* it. I'm not going *anywhere* with you.' She crossed her arms. 'And I'm not lying to Marla.'

'Even if it means helping to secure her future happiness?'

'That's your story. I'd like to think Greg is innocent but...'

That was being naïve, gullible, as her mother had been for too long. Some guys liked it on the side, no matter how devoted they might outwardly appear, her own two-timing father, case in point.

Nate was folding a shirt cuff back up over his wrist...a bronzed, corded forearm. It looked so strong, so lawlessly masculine, she found herself remembering how completely lost she'd felt when they'd kissed this afternoon and, irrespective of knowing that she would never approve of this man, would never agree to anything he might scheme and plan, Roxy found herself asking.

'You want me to abandon my shop and fly off to where exactly?'

'I'm thinking the Outback.'

Her arms unravelled and she sat straighter. 'Really?'

'That appeals?'

'I'd like to experience the red dust and sweeping plains at least once in my life.'

'What about snakes and scorpions?'

'I thought you wanted to talk me into this.'

'Right.' He put on a serious way-too-cute face that sent her pulse rate spiking. 'The carols of kookaburras will wake you each morning, you'll enjoy a panoramic view of rust-coloured hills and fiery sunsets every night, not to mention the magical allure of those endless starry nights. How am I doing?'

She inwardly sighed. *Fabulous.* But it was far from that simple. Remembering her disgust when she'd happened upon the picture of Nate canoodling that woman just days after he'd left her stranded on her doorstep, she pinned her shoulders back and made clear again.

'I only want to do whatever's right for Marla.'

The waiter arrived and poured a wine sample. Nate tasted, voiced his approval and, thoughtful, set his glass down for the waiter to fill.

'Can I ask you something?'

'Thought you already had.'

He ignored her tone and asked, 'Why were you wearing Marla's dress today?'

'I'm a tactile person.' She shrugged. 'I thought wearing the gown, feeling the fabric against my own skin, might help give me an idea or two.'

'More information needed.'

She pressed her lips together, but talking about a bad

situation couldn't make it worse, even if she was talking to a man she didn't trust.

'That dress is entered in a contest,' she admitted. 'First prize includes a showing in Paris, among other fabulous things.'

'And yet you look unhappy.'

'One of the conditions of the contest is that the gown must take its stroll down the aisle by the end of this month. With Marla and Greg's wedding off, so is any chance of that dress taking out the number one spot. Or even a coveted place.'

'What did Marla want you to do with the dress?'

'She doesn't care. As long as she doesn't have to see it again.'

'So someone else could wear it. You could put out an ad or something so long as the nuptials are sealed before the thirty-first.'

'I thought about that, but this dress is special. I couldn't give it away to someone who might not appreciate it.'

'Even for a shot at that contest prize?'

Even if she explained, he wouldn't understand. People didn't value what they got free. What they didn't have to fight for or respect. That gown deserved to be adored.

Besides, 'What if Greg and Marla do get back together?' She collected her water glass. 'Not that I'm saying it'll happen. But in one breath I'm supposed to be working to reunite them and in the next I'm giving her gown away.'

'If those two reunite, all our problems will be solved, *including* your gown's. Greg was caught in an unflattering moment. It can happen to anyone.'

'It's never happened to me.'

He looked as if he might say, *Me either*, but then thought better of it.

'I'm convinced he's meant for Marla and vice versa.'

Nate's glittering gaze took on a distant look. 'A man falls in love only once in his life.'

'Wow. Such conviction. Anyone would think you're an expert.'

'You don't want to know how big of an expert I am.'

Elbows on the table, she set her chin prettily in the net of her thatched fingers. 'But I really, really do.'

That shadowed jaw shifted and he took another sip of wine. He set down the glass, his chest expanded on a breath and he finally said, 'Truth is, I'm the product of a happy family.'

That was it? She sat straighter. 'More information needed.'

'My father fell in love with my mother at first sight,' he went on. 'They married a matter of weeks later. I've always known they were happy together. Were meant to be. The looks they share… Marla and Greg look at each other the same way. It's not something you can fake.'

Roxy's throat swelled. She felt sad and envious as well as pleased for Nate all at the same time. What must it be like to have grown up in such a stable, predictable world and obviously, from Nate's face, not appreciate it nearly enough?

'Must be great to have parents who really get it.' She swallowed as that familiar dark feeling gripped her stomach. 'Think I mentioned my dad's been married three times.'

Nate gestured for the waiter to bring another glass for Marla. 'And your mother?'

'She has a circle of good friends.'

'But none of the male variety?'

'She doesn't believe in love any more.'

'And her daughter creates wedding gowns?'

'My mother supports what I do.' Roxy relented and

sipped her wine, which coursed a warm pleasant path down her throat. 'She often says how proud she is of me.'

'What about you?'

'Of course I'm proud of my career.'

His tone dropped. 'I meant do you believe in marriage?'

The question took Roxy aback. She thought he'd already pegged her as a huge fan—a woman who stuck her claws in at the first opportunity and didn't like to let go. And she wouldn't lie now.

'Pardon the pun but *I do*. I also believe that making it legal shouldn't be rushed.' His eyes took on a new light as those broad shoulders seemed to lock. 'Sounds like your parents lucked out,' she went on, 'but mine married after a whirlwind romance too and they bombed out badly.'

'So it'll be a long engagement for you?'

'I have a career to nurture. Places I want to visit. People I'd like to meet. I'm a long way off from wanting to get serious with someone.' Particularly the *wrong* someone.

'That's exactly how I feel.'

Her grin was wry. 'I kinda guessed.'

As his gaze roamed her face, the awareness glistening in those crystal-cut eyes sent her heartbeat tripping all over itself and her mind wandering to places it shouldn't. She already knew she loved the feel of his mouth on hers, the heat of his amazing body pressed close. She also knew developing feelings for Nate Sparks was completely, totally out of the question. Her mother might have been weak and fallen for a rogue who thought only of himself, but, dammit, she never would.

'I have an idea,' he said, collecting his glass as if ready to make a toast. 'If you agree to be part of this plan and Greg and Marla *don't* make up…'

His head went back as if he were having second thoughts but now, despite it all, she was curious.

'And if they don't make up…?'

'If they don't make up, I'll walk you down the aisle in that dress myself.'

Her vision tunnelled, the world tipped upside down and Roxy forgot to breathe. When she did fill her lungs, it was with a gulp. Then she coughed and had to cover her mouth with the napkin.

'You must have a temperature,' she said over the square of linen. 'You're delirious.'

'You have everything to gain, nothing to lose.'

'Except Marla's friendship when she bans me from her life for deceiving her.'

'I'm betting she'll name their first girl child after you. If not—' his smile softened '—she'll understand. That's what friends do.'

Slowly, Roxy set her napkin down. 'You'd really commit to walking me down the aisle in that dress?'

'It's for a good cause. Besides there's such a thing as annulment.' His laugh was a little too quick. 'We're not talking for real here, Roxy, just a means to an end. We both agreed. Neither of us is after that kind of commitment.'

She blinked and felt her cheeks go horribly warm. Well, of course that was what he'd meant. This proposition was simply another of his angles to get to where he wanted to go.

'Was that a yes?' he asked.

She held her brow. She hadn't said that. She *couldn't* agree. 'That's too wild of an idea.'

'Way I see it, for you it's a safe bet.'

Roxy looked down at her placemat and that big striped cat flashed a challenging grin. Was she like that tiger? Powerful, passionate? *Reckless?* Nate had already said it wouldn't be a *real* wedding…if Marla and Greg didn't make up and it even came to that. One part of her was

shouting, *Do it! He's right. What have you got to lose?*
Another part was shuddering, warning her, *Don't be an
idiot. This can only blow up in your face.*

Roxy gnawed her lower lip, shifted in her seat. 'I don't
know...'

'No decision should be made on an empty stomach.
Let's order and discuss it later. After all—' looking more
commanding and handsome than ever, Nate swept up his
menu '—we have all night.'

Below that ceiling of lanterns an hour later, Nate slid the
leather bill folder the waiter had dropped off over to his
side of the table. 'I'll get this.'

The wallet hadn't left his back pocket before Roxy
swept the folder over to her side.

'We're going Dutch,' she said, curling hair behind an
ear as she concentrated to study the bill.

'I never let a woman pay.'

When he swept the folder back, she sent a dry look that
only made her green eyes sparkle beneath the lighting's
soft glow all the more. 'Nate, don't argue.'

'Going Dutch wasn't the way I was brought up.'

'As old-fashioned as it might sound, if you'd invited
me to dinner for other reasons, I'd let you get the tab. But
this is not a date.'

Her tone said, *As long as I have breath in my body, nor
will there ever be a date.*

She reached again. He caught her hand. The contact
of his skin touching hers sent a surge of blood rushing
through his veins. Low down, he came alive and the part
of him that was plugged into 'me caveman' throbbed and
demanded an audience. The rush of testosterone was natural, uncomplicated. Its intent was also out of the question.

Throughout the evening, and what had turned into a

small banquet, they'd discussed the Outback and had also digressed into travels abroad, ending on federal politics, usually a subject he avoided. People had their own opinion and sometimes a comment could turn into an overly heated, less than pleasant discussion. But he and Roxy shared similar views there too. At one point, he was so engrossed in their discussion regarding new tax implications on fledgling businesses, he forgot the reason they'd met tonight—to sort out their friends' situation. He was sure Roxy had forgotten she was supposed to disapprove of him, which boded well for getting her on board with his plan.

But, Lord above, he should never have touched her. The feel of her hand only made him want to touch more. From the alarm in her wide eyes, Roxy felt the same heat and uncertainty too. Then she did something he couldn't. Her shoulders easing back, she siphoned down a breath and dragged her hand out from beneath his.

'Guess we got sidetracked,' she murmured.

Try as he might, he couldn't take his gaze from her lips. 'Guess we did.'

'Thing is, to get back to it, if I agreed to this Outback plan of yours, Marla would either love me for ever or never talk to me again. When I can't be sure of Greg's intentions that night, I simply can't take that risk.'

Although he capitulated on the bill—they paid half each—he wasn't prepared to accept her decision to bow out of the plan. He meant to convince her and convince her tonight. He simply needed a little more time.

A few minutes later, strolling through Chinatown amid a high-energy Friday night crowd, Nate was focusing on his next move when she stopped at the kerb. Hitching her handbag higher on her shoulder, she raised a hand to flag down an approaching cab. He moved to lower her hand but, remembering that earlier sizzle, thought better of it.

Instead he stated, 'I'll drop you home.'

That cab whizzed by, but she waved at another. 'I can find my own way home.'

'I insist.'

'So do I.'

'I surrendered on the bill,' he pointed out. 'It's your turn to bend.'

'It's not my turn to do anything.'

When a second cab ignored her hail and, stubborn, she only looked for another, he checked out the growing city crowd, then his wristwatch. 'You do realize we could be here all night.'

Roxy opened her mouth to disagree. But then the logic must have interceded because the fire in her eyes faded and eventually she sent a contrite smile in spite of herself. 'Friday night's not the easiest time to get a taxi.'

'No, it's not.'

'Don't suppose you'll take five bucks for gas.'

She was joking. He should laugh. And, truth was, he found her need to be self-sufficient extremely attractive. But the past shaped us all and he wondered if maybe the biggest reason Roxy was Miss Independence now was because she hadn't been able to rely on the person who should have had her back when she was young. Her philandering father. The reason *he* was so driven stemmed back to his father too, but for vastly different reasons.

With traffic whirring by and people rolling past, he stepped forward and smiled down into her beautiful expectant face. Thankfully, she didn't baulk and move away.

'I won't take your money,' he said, 'but you can do something in return.'

A frown pinched her brow. 'Like go to the Outback?'

'I was going to say tell me more about the time you were invited to base-jump in Switzerland.'

Despite the fact she didn't like him—or at least pretended most of the time that was the case—her expression changed now, opened up, and the sparkle he'd seen earlier in her eyes returned.

'By that couple who wanted to spend their honeymoon jumping off cliffs with similar-minded friends,' she clarified. 'Needless to say, I declined.'

'A bat suit not flattering enough?'

'I have a problem with heights.'

As she explained more and they set off for the parking lot, he instinctively went to rest a palm on her back to help guide her through the crowd. At the last moment, he reconsidered. It might be the gentlemanly thing to do, the way he'd been brought up, but as Roxy had said: some risks simply weren't worth taking.

Twenty minutes later, Nate swerved his car in front of Roxy's quaint cottage of a house. The hedges were still maintained, the picket fence still upright and strong. Everything was just as he remembered from six months earlier. Including the sense of physical awareness cracking like an electric whip between them now.

Over the last few minutes, banter had ceased. He couldn't say for sure what she was thinking, feeling. But the only thing rumbling through *his* mind was recalling how he'd felt the last time he'd driven her home. Hyped. Taut with anticipation. That night he'd known he was going to kiss her. He simply hadn't known how darn good it would be.

But he'd already decided he and Roxy would not kiss again. He wasn't ready to take a chance on turning into a hobbled married man overnight like Sparks men were wont to do. Although…

If Roxy was against the idea of settling down as much as he was, didn't that make a difference? Even if the world went mad and he asked her for her hand in a matter of weeks, given what she'd told him earlier, it would only be for the competition. The marriage could be easily dissolved. She was not looking to get tied down. She was a career person, like him.

Nevertheless, when Roxy found the car door release, where he would normally have walked her to the door, Nate stayed glued to his seat. Etiquette was one thing, stupidity versus self-knowledge and survival quite another.

From beneath lowered lashes, she said, 'Thanks for the lift.'

Gripping the steering wheel, he nodded once. 'I'll be in touch.'

'Nate, I am sorry but I—'

Anticipating her words, he cut her off. 'Please. Think about my plan for Marla and Greg overnight. If you're still not convinced, I won't bother you again.'

Did she know he was stretching the truth? Not only was this a good plan, it was the only one he had. With persistence—some subtle persuasion—Roxy would come around.

In the street-lit shadows locked within the car's cabin, her uneasy expression eased and their gazes held for a powerful moment. He gripped the wheel tighter, set his toes into their inner soles more, but that pleasant sensation burning high on his thighs didn't leave him. If she tipped half an inch closer, the fight would be over. He'd have to kiss her—at least just once more. Hell, if she didn't come right out and belt him, kissing her and staying with it might even help his cause.

But then the car door whooshed open and closed and in a blink she was gone, striding down a path that led to her door while the throbbing in all his main arteries pulsed on.

Still, as he watched her retreat, a small smile hooked up on one side of his mouth. He liked the way she walked, particularly in those black tailored trousers. That silk blouse was sexy too. And boots…he'd always been a fan. What kind of lingerie was she hiding beneath that ensemble? He'd bet French lace. *White* sexy-as-hell French lace.

A raucous laugh, loud enough to penetrate his window's glass, grabbed Nate's attention. On the other side of the street, two youths were strutting down the footpath, jeans falling off their backsides, bright coals from cigarettes dangling from their lips. A chill chased up Nate's spine and he shot another glance Roxy's way. Standing outside her front door, she was digging around in her bag for a key. And now those guys had stopped to check out his car. Or were they eyeing the babe standing alone among those convenient shadows?

His heart thudding low in his chest, Nate wrung the steering wheel and waited while Roxy fished around more. When the youths swapped hushed words, laughed again then ambled across to Roxy's side—*his* side—of the street, Nate made an executive decision. He didn't care if those guys were A-grade citizens out for a harmless stroll, which he doubted. He wouldn't leave until Roxy was safe inside.

Nate shoved open the door.

The noise earned the boys' attention. Standing in the cool night air, Nate challenged their wary gaze. After a few seconds, one flicked his butt at the gutter before both continued leisurely past and down the street. Nate almost bared his teeth. *Good riddance and don't come back.*

When the pair was a block away, he focused on Roxy again. Had she lost her keys somewhere? Did she have a spare for the house? He couldn't leave until she was inside, which at this rate might take all night.

As Nate approached the house Roxy pulled her nose out from her bag and her expression opened in surprise.

She stammered, 'Wh-what are you doing?'

'Helping to find your keys.'

'They slipped to the bottom, but I have them now.' She withdrew a set from her bag and jingled.

'Right. Good.' Glancing over his shoulder, Nate craned his neck to be sure that unsavoury element was indeed gone. 'You ought to get inside.' He crowded her back towards the door. 'It's late.'

'I've lived on my own for a while now.'

'Be that as it may.' He took the key she'd chosen from a half-dozen looped on the ring, then unlocked and fanned open the door. 'Remember to lock up behind you.'

Her eyes twinkled with amusement, as if she was less irritated by his edict and maybe more touched.

That menacing laughter rang out again, distant but not nearly far enough away. Hackles rising, Nate headed towards the street to make his presence known again. The Sparks were a family who paid attention to hunches, good and sometimes bad feelings that were in no way limited to choosing a spouse. He trusted his instincts. This one made his gut clutch and the back of his neck go hot.

'Nate?'

He dragged his attention back to where Roxy stood outside her now opened door.

'It's still early,' she said, and her gaze dipped before meeting his again. 'Would you like to come in for a drink?'

At her words, that earlier warmth rose to fill his chest and, for a moment, he couldn't think of one reason he shouldn't. He'd never met a woman he could speak with more easily. He liked her wit, her intelligence, the way that tiny dimple winked in her left cheek whenever she grinned. But if he took up her offer, the night might start with a drink but it sure as heck wouldn't finish on one. Still, she knew now precisely where he stood. And he knew where she stood too. Neither of them wanted 'serious'.

He didn't have to go the whole way and actually *sleep* with her…although some pillow talk leading into the Outback scheme couldn't hurt. But simple truth was—right this minute—he wanted that drink. Wanted that kiss.

'How does coffee sound?' she asked.

'Just coffee?'

'I have hot chocolate. Tea too, I think.'

'Is that all?'

'What else would you like?'

He took two measured steps towards her. 'That's up to you.'

She blinked twice and fast because there was nothing ambivalent about his tone or the intent he was certain shone in his eyes. A small smile quivered on her lips.

'Well, this is a turnaround.'

'Nothing's changed. I wanted to come in that night six months ago too.'

'Except you were dead certain I wanted to throw a rope around your ankles and drag you down the aisle.'

'Now I know better.'

While she peered up uncertainly into his eyes, he soaked up the last of the anticipation, then reached out and took what he couldn't deny either of them a moment more.

CHAPTER THREE

ROXY's head was swimming. In a matter of seconds, a situation she'd had under control had spun a three-sixty and now Nate was going to *kiss* her.

Of course, she'd felt the possibilities—the attraction—building between them all night. Perhaps she'd asked him in because deep down she wanted to face this irresistible force and get it over with. But was she truly game enough to see how long these sparks could fly before multiplying out of control?

She was still angry over the way he'd left her standing here on this very spot six months ago. Still secretly fuming over that photo taken of him enjoying himself with some other woman only a week later. On the other hand, she couldn't deny she'd never felt this strongly about anyone before. She'd never known this kind of intensity existed. Maybe these kinds of feelings were the reason her mother had let her wayward husband come back again and again. Why she'd never had any sense where his obvious shortfalls were concerned. Roxy had been so annoyed by her mother's blindness…her incurable weakness.

Nate's mouth was a hair's-breadth from hers when strength returned to Roxy's legs, she spun around and, still light-headed but seeing more clearly, managed to step over the threshold. Working to catch her breath, she came up with a suitable throwaway line that sounded almost unaffected.

'I think I have some chocolate to go with the coffee.'

'Something sweet sounds good.'

His deep sure tone sent her pulse rampaging all the more. But she didn't want Nate to know the tumult she was in, although by the confident smile she saw smouldering in his eyes when she flicked on the light, she supposed he already knew.

Bolstering herself up, she closed and locked the door, then headed for the kitchen, which was part of the open-plan living area.

'Guess you bring your work home,' he said as she found the coffee grinds and he strolled into a lounge room littered with a designer-slash-seamstress's ware.

'Some might call it messy,' she told him. 'I prefer the term *inspiring*. I have a sewing room here as well as at the shop. Fabric, patterns, lace and buttons… It all kind of spills out around the place.'

Edging around two partially dressed mannequins, he pretended to shudder. 'I feel like I'm being watched.'

'Wait till they start talking to you.'

He shot her a wry glance. 'Just assure me you don't talk back.'

Roxy didn't admit that, late at night on a deadline, sometimes she thought they did.

While she thumbed on the kettle and worked to rationalise her feelings—what she truly wanted from tonight, why she wanted it, whether she was in any way like her mother—Nate wandered around more.

'Where do you get your ideas?'

'I keep abreast of present fashions as well as past.' She flicked the tap and rinsed the plunger out. 'When I'm commissioned to design a dress, I try hard to get inside the bride's skin, so to speak. Understand what tone she wants to relay and capture it as closely as I can.'

Looking larger than life in her usually uncomplicated space, Nate had stopped to study a magazine spread on spring brides opened on the couch. He ran a hand through his coal-black hair as he leaned forward to focus more on the page.

'Ever get it wrong?' he asked, leaving the magazine to head for the kitchen where she was pouring boiled water.

'I had a client once who wanted to look like a bunny.'

'As in Playboy or Bugs?'

'As in big front teeth, carrot loving, fluffy ball of tail. We talked extensively and I came up with sketches and ultimately a gown I thought captured her dream about her walk, or should I say *hop*, down the aisle.'

'Then she decided to go as Bambi, right?'

'Oh, no. This woman was focused. Picture it. A winter theme. The bolero jacket lovingly sewn from imitation fur. A veil that, as best I could manage, resembled bunny ears. A fluffy ball secured the train at the back.'

'And she hated it.'

'She loved it!' Roxy set the mugs, sugar and some cream on a tray. 'In fact, it wasn't enough. She wanted whiskers attached to the veil. You know, the part that covers a bride's face before the groom kisses her.'

'Forgive me for saying, but, *Wacko*.'

She plunged the coffee. 'I said I could do the whiskers… somehow. But then she had another brilliant idea. A bouquet of fresh carrots and she wanted all the guests to wear carrot buttonholes and corsages.'

'Like I said…' He wound a finger around near his temple before moving to help with the tray.

She indicated he should set it on the coffee table and admitted, 'The groom had had enough.'

Roxy lowered down on one side of the three-seater while Nate took the couch's other end—a relatively safe distance from each other, although given how close he'd come to capturing her on the doorstep a few minutes ago, she wasn't certain that would last, or whether she really wanted it to. With a remarkably steady hand, she poured his coffee and handed it over.

'This guy said he loved her carrot cake and fluffy bunny feet slippers, but no way was *he* wearing carrots. Enough was enough. The disagreement escalated. The wedding was called off. The bride wouldn't blame her fiancé or herself so she blamed me for not delivering.'

He frowned before his gaze filled with disbelief, then compassion. 'You're serious.'

'It's not up to me to tell a bride what her expectations of her big day should be—' she had her own ideas…romantic, tastefully unique '—but I've learned that sometimes it's best to follow instinct and suggest perhaps another designer.'

While stirring in sugar, he cast another curious look around and Roxy forced her focus away from the rhythmic motion of his hand and how that smattering of dark hair filtering down one side made her feel a little weak and definitely wanting. Which was a far cry from the stand she'd taken over the preceding six months when she'd sworn they would never lock lips again.

Concentrating to fill her mug and contain her see-sawing feelings, she passed another look over the fabric samples and mannequins, and frowned. They really were everywhere.

'This must look incredibly unnecessary to someone who doesn't know how to thread a needle.'

'So you presume.'

About to sip, she arched a brow. 'Don't tell me you know how to sew?'

'My mother tried to teach me to hem once. She said domestic chores weren't purely women's work.'

'What did your dad say?'

'I think he was busy ironing at the time.'

Roxy chuckled. 'Did you learn to hem?'

'I'm relieved to say she gave up on me. Threading that eensy-weensy needle near drove me mad.'

A common dilemma. She set down her mug. 'Let me introduce you to a common trick of the trade.'

After sourcing a needle from a nearby sewing box, as well as a length of thread and her trusty needle threader, she moved to sit on the padded arm of the couch nearest Nate, but then stopped. Wasn't she inviting trouble?

On the other hand—if she put a zipper on the voice inside her head—wasn't a teeny taste of trouble what she wanted?

Implements in hand, she shored herself up and set her behind down on the padded couch arm. She angled slightly so that her doubtful student could see every step.

'You slot this looped wire through the eye of the needle, like so.'

His head going back, Nate squinted. 'See. Right there. Already I need a magnifying glass.'

'You'll never thread a needle any other way after this.'

'I'll never thread a needle again, period.' Gifting her a dazzling grin that made her insides squeeze and quiver, he took the needle, the threader. He shut one eye, pulled his mouth a certain scrumptious way and poked the wire through. Chuffed, he sat back. 'Now what?'

'Run the thread through the opening of the looped wire.'

One eye closed again, he guided the thread through, then let out a deeply satisfied sigh. 'Next?'

'You pull the threader back through the eye of the needle and it's done.'

'It can't be that simple.'

She'd been concentrating on the threader, on the process. But now she felt her hand lightly touching his—or, more precisely, that sexy smattering of dark hair—and a tingling bright sensation fell through her middle, settling into an all too pleasant heat at her core. Had Nate noticed that her breathing was coming slightly faster, that she was leaning that bit closer?

As her heartbeat rushed in her ears, carefully she lifted her gaze.

Nate was looking not at the needle and thread but at her. From the smoke in his usually clear blue eyes, he'd guessed at her avalanche of feelings. When a pulse beat once low on his cheek and he tipped closer, his gaze gravitating to her lips, the brushfires coursing through her blood threatened to turn into an inferno. A knowing grin lifted a corner of his mouth while his gaze stroked her like a lover's touch.

'Nope. I still can't quite seem to get it…'

Short on air, Roxy managed to swallow. Damn the man. Neither could she. Did he want to kiss her or not?

He must have read her mind. Blindly he set the needle and thread on the coffee table, then one big palm curled around her nape while the other cupped her shoulder, winging her gently in. His head angled and gaze intensified as if he was giving her time to truly grasp what was about to unfold, then his essence seemed to fill every part of her, her eyes drifted closed and his mouth at last met hers.

That familiar drugging warmth filtered through her system as Roxy slipped into a state of both blessed relief and spiralling passion while the wet tip of his tongue traced over her lower lip, then slid past her teeth to wind deep and hot inside. With him holding and exploring her, her arms went out to draw him in at the same time any oxygen left in her world evaporated and she surrendered without reserve. As much as she'd like to deny it—deny him—wasn't this the moment she'd been waiting for?

As she savoured the embrace and his chin grazed her cheek, he manipulated her around until she'd drifted to lie near horizontal, draped over his lap. With one palm cradling her head and his chest rumbling with satisfaction, he proceeded to kiss her more thoroughly than she'd ever been kissed before. Still she needed more.

Drowning in sensation, she reached across, found the hand gripping her shoulder and slid his palm down her upper arm, then over towards her breast. When his fingertips brushed the peak beneath her blouse, her womb compressed and beat a rhythm that released a hot surge of longing at the apex of her thighs. He rolled and plucked the sensitive tip until the throbbing in her belly grew to a point where she only wanted to rip off her clothes and have him finish feeding this mind-blowing want. It was official. She'd lost her mind.

But then the crush of his kiss eased enough for him to murmur against her parted lips.

'Mmm…this *is* sweet.' His smile feathered over her mouth. 'Very sweet, indeed.'

His mouth claimed hers again while that hand ironed down her side, over the ticklish slope near her hip and across to that part of her that begged for attention. Over the fabric of her trousers, his long fingers curved down and pressed between her legs. When she melted more, his touch rode slightly higher to circle a spot that felt three heartbeats away from catching light and consuming her whole. Her every cell floated higher while her core squeezed and pulsed and reality shrank down to only this. To only Nate and only now.

When the pressure of his touch, of his kiss, lightened again, Roxy groaned as some of what the world had been before filtered in. She couldn't care if Hollywood's most celebrated female celebrity were knocking on her door desperate for a million-dollar dress. Her only thought was to have him back. Have him kiss her again and again.

His scratchy cheek came to rest alongside hers as his deep velvet voice rumbled at the sensitive shell of her ear.

'I'm glad we worked out our differences.'

His mouth gravitated to her throat and nibbled down while she sighed and murmured, 'Me too.'

'I vote we take this to your bedroom.' His tongue looped around the hollow at the base of her throat. 'Call me cautious but I'm not a friend of stray needles.'

Spreading her fingers over his shoulder, she arched towards him and, as if the world were about to end and this would be their last, he scooped under her back, lifted her higher and kissed her again. The raw sensation he mined from deep inside left her mind blank but for the stars. His next words were muffled and rough as he spoke against her lips as if he couldn't bear to leave them.

'Which way?'

She was prying his shirt tails out from beneath his belt. 'Which way what?'

She felt his grin. 'Your bedroom.'

Oh, yes… She hummed out a smile. She longed to sprawl out on cool sheets while he flicked open her blouse buttons, wound the silk from her shoulders, peeled the bra from her…*from her*…

A sudden heart-stopping fright seized her chest and Roxy's eyes flew open as ice-cold dread fell like a lead weight through her middle. She'd totally forgotten. Beneath her blouse, her chemise, she wore underwear a prim great-aunt would be ashamed of. She couldn't let him see her in granny pants. But now they'd come this far, what could she do or say to get around it? Maybe if they went to the bedroom and kept the lights off…

She blinked and came back to the here and now. Nate was peering down at her most curiously. Her face beginning to burn, Roxy eased up and sat alongside him while he studied her face, then carefully cupped her cheek.

'You went all stiff,' he said. 'Did I do something wrong?'

'No.' *God, no!* 'I was just thinking, ah…thinking that I should, um…' She searched her panicked brain, gave a quick smile and a shrug. 'That I should go freshen up.'

'Well, sure.' He cleared his throat, siphoned down a settling breath, then looked at her closer still. 'Roxy, are you sure everything's okay? Because if you're uncomfortable with us getting together like this—without any added strings, I mean—tell me. I'd rather know.'

She took in the earnest slant of his brows, the cautionary tone in his voice, and more of those glorious got-to-have-you feelings fragmented and floated away. Pulling her mouth to one side, she brushed hair back from her face and replied.

'Nate, I don't need to be told that this is sex for sex's sake.'

His expression softened as his eyes dropped to stroke her lips once more. 'You know that's not the way I see this.'

In a skilled fluid movement, he angled to bring her against him again. But a flattened palm against his hard chest stopped him dead. She needed to know.

'How *do* you see this?'

'As two like-minded people moving forward, coming together.' His hot mouth brushed and tickled her ear. 'Hopefully coming a lot.'

Cute. But not the answer she was looking for.

When a knuckle drew a confident line up her throat and urged her chin back—when she found her mouth a breath away from his again—unease rose higher, her throat closed off and, decided, she got to her feet. Straightening her blouse, she tried to gather her jumbled thoughts. One day he was running and the next he was all over her, but making doubly sure that she knew this meant nothing beyond the physical. A quick romp in the sack. No doubt the same kind of tumble he'd enjoyed with that brunette from the photo, and how many more since.

'Is this how you treat every woman you're attracted to?'

He looked insulted. 'Of course not.'

'Then why *me*?'

'Because, unless you hadn't noticed, I'm not simply attracted to you.' A line formed between his brows before he rubbed his palms up and down his long hard thighs. 'It's complicated.'

'Unlike a quick shag in my bed tonight.'

'No, actually, that *is* complicated.' His gaze and voice dropped. 'More complicated than you could imagine.'

To keep her heart from dropping any lower, she knotted her arms over her waist. 'I need some answers, Nate, and I need them fast.'

'You wouldn't believe it.'

Her eyes narrowed. 'Try me.'

He squared his shoulders, rubbed his thighs again.

'If you really want to know,' he said, 'my family is cursed, although *cursed* is an interchangeable term. My parents and grandparents would say that we're blessed.'

She edged away. 'Okay. Now you're freaking me out. Do you all turn into snarling wolves on a full moon?'

'Only Great-uncle Stuart on my mother's side.' Her mouth dropped open and he grinned. 'Now you can laugh.'

She glared but refrained from telling him to forget she'd ever asked. A curse. Well, at least he had imagination.

'Go on,' she said. 'I'm listening. Although I'm not certain why.'

'From as far back as anyone can remember,' he said, pushing to his feet, 'Sparks men have been hit hard when Cupid's arrow strikes.'

'That doesn't sound so tragic to me. In fact, it sounds rather romantic.'

'Romantic, lucky, decisive. All those things and, apparently, all good for those who have come before me. Dad, Grandfather Sparks and on up the line…they've all fallen and for the right woman, it would seem. Each couple has tied the knot within weeks of starting to date. Nine months on, like clockwork, the first child comes along, and any plans for a career, for a solid future, is put on the back burner indefinitely. My father could have been a surgeon. Instead for years he cleaned bedpans.'

'And that's the curse's fault?'

His chiselled features hardened more. 'My predecessors have given up everything for love. Career. Health. In some instances, their sanity. Call me selfish or an egotist but I don't want to be a hospital wardsman or the road maintenance guy who holds up slow-down signs when I can work in a professional field that I'm good at. That I enjoy.'

Roxy eyed him up and down. This was hogwash. Curses weren't real. Intelligent men weren't bewitched by women who sucked out their souls. This must be another scam, like when, earlier, he'd manipulated Ava Morris into believing he was a genuine guy with a fiancée he adored. Having said that, she would concede she was beyond grateful for the sale. At least she could pay some outstanding bills.

And yet as she continued to study him Roxy couldn't help but be halfway convinced by the resignation shining in his eyes. Could he have been brainwashed from child-hood into accepting this family curse junk? Common sense wasn't a factor when you were taught from birth what to believe. What was truth. Like, *Your father does love us. If he didn't, he wouldn't come back.*

'This has really got you convinced, hasn't it?'

'I grew up dirt poor,' he said, 'which I can more than handle. The really hard part was having a father who couldn't function without his other half. I'm saying if my mother had died, he would have died too. When you have five kids to consider, I don't care how many love stories you've seen, that's not romantic. It's—'

Growling, he bit off the word.

'You're the only son,' she said. *The oldest.* 'What do your sisters say?'

'They never had careers to consider. And before you pounce, my respect for a woman doesn't hinge on whether she has a career or not. I'm just saying.'

Being the only other 'man' in the family, perhaps Nate felt the responsibility—the link with his parents—more deeply or differently than the girls. She had to ask.

'Sure there's not a little Oedipus syndrome going on here?'

He pulled a pained face. 'But even if there were, fact remains, I'm not ready to settle down. Fall in love. Gamble my future or throw it away.'

Her smile was thin. *Nice.* 'I pity the poor girl you end up proposing to—properly, that is.'

'That's a long way off.'

She studied the firm set of his mouth and for a heart-beat she wanted to comfort him. Seemed his childhood wasn't as rosy as she first thought. He'd grown up feeling pushed to the background. Feeling as if he and his siblings didn't matter as much as they should. At least when her father had been home, he'd showered her with affection. Her dad was a charismatic man, the kind who didn't self-analyze or register any guilt.

But as much as Roxy sympathized with 'Nate the boy', a stronger part of her said, *Enough*. A whole new stream of commitment phobia could be named after 'grown-up Nate'. Whether he was justified in his negative stand regarding love and marriage, she wasn't in a position to say. She hadn't lived his life and didn't own anyone's opinions. She could only look after her own best interests and more than ever they seemed clear.

Roxy shored herself up. 'It's certainly been an interesting evening.'

The tension in his face, in his stance, seemed to ease. A grateful smile hooked one corner of his mouth at the same time long warm fingers curled around her hand and, just like that, a bevy of sparks spiralled up her arm, stole her breath.

'So you *do* understand,' he said.

'Frankly, I'm not sure if I do or I don't. I only know I don't feel as convinced about having you stay as I did five minutes ago.'

On a logical level, she knew that at this point in their lives neither wanted anything as serious as marriage. But she simply couldn't sleep with someone who made it sound as if she was little more than a release for sexual cravings. Yes, she'd been as turned on as Nate, but, now that she'd had time to take a breath, she knew this scenario was all wrong. She wasn't after phone calls every night; however, neither would she accept, *Thanks for the hump. I'll call if I call.* That was too darn close to the treatment her mother had accepted. She had more respect for herself than that.

His grip and jaw tightened even as his grin grew and

he joked. 'I could go with the curse turning me into a wolf if that'd help.'

She couldn't see anything would.

Feeling flat but resigned, she slipped her hand away from his. 'I need for you to go.'

CHAPTER FOUR

SITTING on the verandah of Marla's third-storey apartment late the next day, Roxy slid another Scrabble tile onto the game board and in a supportive tone asked her friend the question that had hung in the air since she'd arrived.

'How are you holding up?'

'All things considered...' Absently studying the board, which had been handed down through her family from the fifties, Marla shrugged. 'It'll take a while.'

'Have you heard from Greg?'

'Not since that slideshow.'

Greg running slides of their most romantic moments from a projector onto a screen outside her apartment had been an inventive way to reach Marla when she wouldn't take his calls. The upshot, however, was that the shots had reminded Marla of those despised pictures she'd seen on the Net. She'd been less than impressed.

'Greg broke my heart,' Marla went on. 'I don't know if I'll ever trust a man again. I wanted to spend the rest of my life with him, have children together.' Shaking back her auburn locks, she put more steel into her voice. 'I can't believe he was groping a near-naked woman behind my back, and who knows what else? A lot more happens at those buck's nights than some women might think. A *lot* more.'

Surrounded by sweet-smelling umbrellas of Jacaranda blooms, Roxy mulled over Marla's heartbreaking situation as well as Nate's suggestion they ought to get the couple together to give them time to sort it out. When she'd asked Nate to leave last night, Roxy had been determined that would be the last she'd ever hear of him or that plan, and Marla's response now only validated her decision. Her friend needed time to heal, not a web of lies that would hurl her into the face of the person who had shredded her heart.

Good or bad, images stuck. Heck, *Marla* had never been snapped fondling another person's private parts.

Although…

Roxy remembered at the hen's night, as part of the show, a nicely built topless waiter had flirted with the bride-to-be unashamedly and Roxy had laughed and cheered as hard as the rest. What would Greg say if he were to watch a tape of that? Was it a once-in-a-lifetime situation, a bit of harmless fun or something best kept concealed? One day when the right man came along, no doubt she would enjoy a hen's night too.

But if what Nate said was true, a Sparks man didn't care to celebrate a buck's night so much as make a commitment to the woman he adored. And in truth, despite being annoyed, frustrated—hurt—Roxy had to wonder. When he got over his angst and did allow himself to fall in love, would Nate make a devoted husband? Someone a wife could be proud to have at her side? Would it be a case of 'like Sparks father like Sparks son'?

Each deep in their own thoughts, the women played a few more words before Marla spoke again.

'I wasn't going to tell you until plans were set, but it's only a matter of a week or so now.'

Curious, Roxy glanced up from collecting more tiles. 'What plans?'

'I'm leaving the country. I've told you about my brother and his IT firm in California. He suggested I go stay with him a while. Learn something different. Make new friends.' Marla reached over and caught Roxy's arm. 'Not that I don't value the ones I have here.' She tried to smile. 'You understand, don't you, Rox?'

Feeling giddy, Roxy had to sit back. She knew, despite the distance, Marla was close to her brother, but this decision had left her reeling.

'How long will you be gone?'

'A year. Two.' Marla shrugged. 'I'm not sure.'

On one hand Roxy was pleased Marla had decided to take a firm grip on life's reins and move forward. Neither of them was the type to wallow in self-pity and, given that Marla earned a living as a freelance business consultant, she didn't have any concrete employment ties. On the other, Roxy would miss her friend like crazy. They did so much together, had shared so much.

And there was Greg, a man who had pledged his innocence…just as Roxy's father always had.

But was it possible that Nate was right? What if Greg *had* been a victim of circumstance and he and Marla could get over this major bump in their road? That would never happen with ten thousand miles and two years or more separating them.

Until a moment ago, she'd been better than okay with letting matters take their own course. But with Marla deciding to leave—and so soon—suddenly the way ahead didn't seem quite so clear.

Roxy set down the last tile in her word—an *H*—and summoned the courage to ask. 'What if you woke up tomorrow morning and found out it had all been a horrible mistake. That Greg hadn't done anything wrong and you could still go ahead with the wedding?'

Her eyes glistening, Marla sighed. 'If that were to happen, if I could somehow truly find that faith again and get those pictures out of my mind…well, I'd be the happiest, most relieved woman in the world.'

Then, with a wan smile, she set down three letters after Roxy's. The word spelled HOPE.

'You *have* to come to the anniversary party. Mum and Dad will be crushed if you don't.'

Nate turned away from his sister—the second eldest of the Sparks siblings—to resume a seat at his apartment's dining room table; he'd been sorting out reports before Ivy's unexpected visit. He didn't mind being interrupted. He simply felt uncomfortable about the reason.

'I never said I *wouldn't* go.' He dragged over a pile of papers. 'It's just I probably won't stay long.'

'If you have a hot date lined up, bring her.'

'I don't have a hot date.'

'Then maybe you should find one.'

He sent her a look. 'Don't start on me about finding a nice girl and settling down. I get enough of that from our father.'

'I'm not talking about *till death us do part*.' Ivy's blue-grey eyes filled with needless sympathy. 'I'd simply like to see you get out from under your grindstone and let your hair down a bit. We all would. You've been so focused on getting this business of yours off the ground, you barely take time to eat.'

'I eat. *And* I have a personal life.'

She arched an eyebrow and looked over the papers. 'So, what's this you're busy with?'

'I'm sorting out performance charts for reps as a function of purchasing patterns and meeting bi-annual budgets.'

Ivy emptied her lungs. 'The perfect way to spend a

Sunday.' She crossed her arms over the waist of her pink cotton dress and pegged out a leg. 'When was the last time you went out to dinner? And I'm talking attractive female, not wheeling and dealing with some boring businessman type.'

'Businessmen aren't boring,' he eyed his colour-coded charts and mumbled, '...necessarily.'

'So when?'

'As a matter of fact, I took a lady out night before last.'

Ivy's gaze sharpened. 'Have you seen her before?'

'Affirmative.'

'Plan to see her again?'

He thought for a moment and admitted, 'I'd like to.' Irrespective of the disappointing way the night had ended—how much Roxy obviously still didn't trust him—simple truth was he'd like to a lot.

'Ohmigod.' Ivy sank into the chair beside him. 'It's serious.'

'Don't go choosing bridesmaid's shoes just yet. I would never let it get that far.' *And neither would Roxy.*

Before tossing him out, she'd made herself clear. Roxy was attracted to him physically, intellectually, but she didn't want to rub shoulders with his demons. Perhaps she thought he used his family history as an excuse, a trick so she wouldn't expect him to call—at least not regularly.

He hadn't stopped thinking about her since and, for the first time in years, he was questioning his beliefs. Still, curse or not, he did *not* want to get hitched. But he *did* want to spend time with the woman who his mind respected and his body craved—more every minute.

'So, will the family meet this mystery girl at the anniversary dinner?' Ivy asked. 'I mean before you whisk her off somewhere quiet and romantic, away from your terribly supportive dreary family?'

Shoving the reports aside, he moved to a glass slider's view of Sydney's cityscape and Harbour Bridge. 'She's not going to that party.'

Even if he did decide to brave the endless questions from family members—their over-the-top encouragement—and ask her, Roxy wouldn't accept.

Ivy sniffed. 'Anyone might think you're ashamed of us.'

'You know that's not true. It'll be the same old crowd going over the same old stories. The food will be more extravagant, the fireworks brighter and higher, but the couple of the moment will still be trying to set me up with some woman or other. Drives me *nuts*.'

They'd grown up poor but five years ago a distant relative had left his mother a stack of money, so the anniversary parties were the same—only *bigger*.

Ivy grinned as she had when they were kids and she beat him at checkers. 'They won't try to set you up if you bring someone of your own along. I for one am dying to meet her. What does she do for a living? Blonde or brunette? Is she wildly in love with you already or playing it cool?'

'Depends which day it is.' When Ivy's ears seemed to prick, Nate waved his hands. *Scrap that*. But he did have something he wanted to share or, rather, ask. A question that had eaten at him since leaving Roxy's place so abruptly Friday night.

'Ivy, what do you know about the Sparks family curse?'

'Don't call it that. It's a—'

'Blessing. Right. What do you know?'

'It stems from an epitaph Great-grandfather Sparks found on an ancestor's gravestone back in England. Read something like…*"I live only for your heart and wither without your love."* The wife was buried one day, her husband a month later. More ancestral research led our great-grandfather to the conclusion that we have a history of falling in love quickly and staying that way.' Her sigh eased into a soft faraway smile. 'I get such a buzz from telling the kids how Nan and Grandad fell in love at first sight just like a prince and princess from a fairy tale.'

'Our grandparents too,' he said, crossing back from the view.

'Don't you melt whenever you see those two walking hand in hand? I hope Cameron and I are still cuddling when we're eighty-five.'

Nate didn't doubt Ivy and her husband would be. Those two adored each other, and their two children. Another happy family Sparks success story. But that wasn't what he wanted to know.

'So, is there anything in it? Is the curse real or not?'

She blinked and then her eyes widened to saucers. 'You *are* serious about this girl, aren't you? You're afraid you'll beg for her hand, the curse, as you call it, will be awakened and all the effort you've put into this business hope will come to nothing because you'd have found something that matters more than money.'

He held onto his groan and asked again. 'Do you think there's some kind of voodoo involved or it's just a matter of, well…emotion?'

'Maybe it's both.' Gazing down, she twirled the gold band circling a finger on her left hand. 'Falling in love is a magical experience.'

He sat down at the table again. 'There's nothing magical about wearing patches to school.'

'Your pants may have been patched from time to time but it was a good school. A *private* school. You got a great education, Nate. We all did.'

'It wouldn't have been such an almighty struggle if Dad had finished his own education.'

'I imagine children from divorced families struggle more than we did. Money was tight—'

'We couldn't afford to have the phone on. The electricity sometimes.'

'Which is an even greater testimony to our parents' dedication.'

What about their father's obsession with their mother to a point where nothing else mattered? Husband, fathers, were meant to be strong. Why couldn't his father have been a man as well as an enamoured spouse?

'I guess you and I see things differently,' Ivy said. 'Maybe because I'm happily married and...'

When her lips pressed together and her gaze veered off, he prodded.

'And what?'

She shrugged. 'I'm sorry, Nate. It's not something a person can explain.'

He assessed his sister's pitying smile and growled, not at her as much as himself. Would he still be torn this way at forty, fifty, *sixty*? He wanted to have a family some day, just not before he'd set himself up. Before he'd achieved what he'd worked so hard to secure.

Although, he shouldn't forget that Roxy felt the same way. She wasn't after a gold ring. But he also knew, despite her stand the other night, she wanted to spend time with him as much as he wanted to spend time with her.

Ten minutes later, Ivy was saying her goodbyes and Nate was still thinking about Roxy. Maybe he would call. He could pretend to keep busy, pretend he could forget, but the truth was he needed to talk with her again. Talk... and more.

Dammit, he couldn't get away from the fact that he wanted to know Roxy in the most intimate way. He wanted to make love to her—fiercely, then slowly, then all night long. Even now he could feel the satin of her skin beneath his fingers as his hands moulded over her bare limbs, her belly. Her breasts. Awake half the night, staring at the ceiling, he'd imagined the secret taste of her and how she might arch up and grip her legs around his thighs at the same time he lowered and plunged into her damp sweet warmth.

Ivy was right about one thing. He *did* need a hot date.

He needed Roxy.

He was saying goodbye to his sister at the door when his phone beeped with a text. Nate checked the ID and near fell over.

I'LL PROBABLY REGRET THIS, the message read, BUT GUESS I'M IN. It was signed ROXY T.

CHAPTER FIVE

Two days later, Roxy and Marla arrived in the red dry plains of Australia's Outback.

From Sydney they'd flown north to Brisbane to board a small aircraft, which had taken just the two of them into the centre of Queensland. Nate had organised a later private flight for himself and Greg. All very clandestine. Another word that came to Roxy's mind was *underhanded*. She was still in two minds as to whether she ought to have given in and agreed.

After their Scrabble game and Marla's admission that she wished those photos and her doubts regarding Greg were somehow a mistake, Roxy had confirmed she'd go along with Nate's plan—but she was far from comfortable. Whether it was sweet-talking her customers or working his way around her and almost into her bed, Nate was a master manipulator. She only had to think of her parents' relationship to know a man's charm—even declarations of love—could be turned on and off to suit. But she wasn't here to dwell on that.

As the four-wheel-drive transfer vehicle pulled up now outside what would be their lodgings for the next few days, she only hoped that Nate's faith in his friend was true and well founded, and a happy ending would justify these deceptive means. She could only pray that her friend would make the right decision for her. And, hey, maybe Marla *would* say 'I do' and wear the gorgeous gown specially created for the occasion…the gown that might make that contest deadline after all.

With a hot breeze blowing in her face and a blazing midday sun beating down, Roxy alighted from the vehicle to study the eerily quiet landscape and sprawling, obviously once-grand but presently wholly unglamorous, homestead.

'I appreciate the surprise,' Marla said, 'but when you asked me to push back my plans for California to fit in a girlie escape to a secret location, I expected a tropical island. You know? Lying on some powdery beach, sipping a creamy cocktail.' She swiped at a noisy fly. 'Why this place?'

Roxy took in the homestead's flaky paint then a Frilly lizard scrambling over a bed of dead flowers and tried to make light. Not the Hilton, but didn't the charm of this old homestead make their trip more…interesting?

'Didn't you ever want to experience kangaroos bounding free? The enormous majesty of an Outback sunset?' She recited a couple of lines from a famous poem about a sun-burned country and sweeping plains. 'Who knows how long you'll be in California? This might be your only chance to experience your native country's true character.'

'I don't plan to be gone for ever.' Ducking, Marla waved away another pea-sized fly. 'Just long enough to escape for a while. To forget.'

When Marla's eyes welled and she slid the sunglasses perched atop her head onto her nose to hide the glisten of tears, Roxy tried to swallow the lump swelling in her own throat. Since they'd met in university, she and Marla had been as close as sisters; being an only child from an unstable home, that meant a lot. Too much to lose. And yet here she was jeopardizing that relationship. Then again, this might pay off in the best way possible and make their friendship even stronger.

Roxy held her swooping stomach. God, how she wished everything about this time were over.

At the same time the vehicle pulled away, the homestead's screen door squeaked open and a couple in their fifties moved out onto the wide verandah that surrounded the entire length of the house. The silver-haired man wore pressed jeans, a checkered shirt and a warm smile. In a faded printed dress, his beaming wife held onto his arm until the couple was close enough to extend a hand to greet their city guests.

'I'm Celia Glenrowan,' the woman said, and Roxy shook her weathered hand after Marla. 'Welcome to Glenrowan Station.'

'Celia can show you to your rooms,' Mr Glenrowan said, filing back hair before placing a battered Akubra square on his head. 'Then we can have a bite to eat and maybe take a ride around. You girls know how to handle a horse?'

Roxy spoke for them both. 'I do. I'm sure Marla would love to learn.'

'We got a couple of real ladies that'll suit you both just fine,' Mrs Glenrowan said, heading back to the homestead.

Mr Glenrowan collected the luggage. 'We'll keep the stallions for the other guests. Think the man said they liked to ride hard.'

Marla's brows lifted. 'There's other guests?'

'Due later today,' Mr Glenrowan replied, following his wife.

Marla murmured to Roxy, 'As long as it's not a couple of bad boys on the prowl. Then again, that type usually hit the hot spots—' she plucked at her blouse '—and I don't mean Simpson Desert hot.'

Roxy hid a cringe as her guilt barometer hit an all-time high. While an unsuspecting Marla headed off after the Glenrowans, she took in another sweeping glance over the gum-tree-studded panorama before folding her sleeves up another turn, saying a quick prayer and following.

The last through that screen door, Roxy was apparently the first to hear the churning rumble filtering in from afar. Cupping a hand over her brow, she squinted through the haze and spied a four-wheel-drive hovering on the shimmering horizon. She didn't think she or Marla had left anything behind but had their driver spotted something that he was good enough to want to return? Except the approaching vehicle was red whereas theirs had been white—which meant more visitors?

They four were supposed to be the only guests, but Nate and Greg weren't due for another two hours. Still, as the vehicle rumbled closer Roxy couldn't shake the feeling that one of its occupants was indeed her accomplice in crime. Perspiration beaded across her forehead and her thoughts began to race.

She and Nate had talked over the phone at length about arrangements, including the fact she'd secured the services of her younger cousin, who was in between jobs and grateful for the opportunity to mind the store for some extra cash. But they hadn't discussed a plan B should they land here at the same time. She and Marla were meant to be taking a tour around the property when the boys arrived.

Feeling queasy, Roxy stepped back from the door. Greg was in trouble because of his alleged subterfuge. Roxy could make excuses for herself—for this—but was she really any better?

Soon the vehicle pulled up. The driver let the engine run while Greg jumped down from the back seat, overnighter in hand. Having exited the other side, Nate rounded the tailgate. In such a harsh setting, under such intense circumstances, the sight of him took Roxy's breath away.

Walking into her shop the other day, he'd cut an impressive figure in a dark, tailored suit. In chinos and a more casual white button-down that night, he'd looked so hot, the sight of him had left her parched. But today—*now*— her every thought, every cell, was drawn to the uncompromising masculine sight of him. She wanted to tell herself that she couldn't stand the sight of him. But that would be the biggest lie of all.

When a simple chambray shirt, cuffs folded halfway up two tanned forearms, covered *that* broad chest and shoulders, it was transformed into something extraordinary. Watching those light blue jeans hug his thighs as he sauntered around the vehicle left her feeling giddy. By the time a black Akubra was fitted atop dark hair that ruffled in a rippling breeze, her heart was hammering double time up near her throat. Suddenly she was consumed by thoughts of the sensations he'd so effortlessly brought out in her the other night…feelings that had left her boneless, yearning to have him naked, hard and unapologetically close.

Why did he have to be so screwed up about curses and blessings and drag her into the mix?

She watched as Nate took in the bordering straggly gums and a drunken wire fence that disappeared into a drowsy infinity before shaking hands with the driver through the opened window, then saluting him off. A moment later, the vehicle rolled away, churning plumes of red dust in its wake. Roxy's stomach churned too. Was she meant to stand here, frozen, waiting for Marla to wander out and the bomb to fall? She'd rather dig a hole and disappear for good.

In a deep wry voice, Greg said to Nate, 'Could you have taken us anywhere more remote?'

'The idea was to get away.' Nate moved forward with the gait of a man expecting to step on a landmine any minute. He must feel as anxious as she did.

'Look, I know you're worried about the business,' Greg said, following, 'but you don't need me to make that company of yours a success.'

'That's one man's opinion.' Nate broke into a smile and clapped his buddy on the back. 'Let's get these bags inside and see what's what.'

Roxy shut her eyes as her stomach swooped again. This was the moment. Rather than them run into her here, hiding, better she get her butt out there and face the music now.

At the same time she pushed at the screen door Marla came up behind her and Roxy jumped and swallowed a surprised yelp.

'Our rooms are gorgeous,' Marla said. 'So big and comfy-looking. What's keeping you?' She must have seen the dread in her friend's face and, worried, she lowered her voice. 'Roxy, what's wrong? You look ready to faint.'

Roxy held her friend's shoulders. 'There's something I need to tell you. And before I do, I want you to know that there's nothing I wouldn't do for you. You know that, right?'

At that moment, Marla must have heard the men speaking, recognized the voices, then immediately dismissed it all as imagination because her expression went from worry to alarm to self-reproach in the blink of an eye. But when those voices grew louder, closer, Marla frowned and stepped around Roxy to peer out through the screen door. A heartbeat later, she made a sound as if she'd been kicked in the gut at the same time her knees gave way; Roxy had to dive to hold her friend up before she crumpled to the floor. Together they gazed out as the men strolled nearer, chatting, laughing, although, to someone in the know, Nate's body language seemed guarded.

Marla didn't consult her friend. Rather she straightened and burst through the door. Marla was a deeply feeling person but she could also be steely tough when the situation demanded. It was one of the reasons Roxy respected her so much. And why she was so worried now.

When Greg saw Marla, his smile slipped from his face and his lazy pace ground to a halt at the same time his head slanted to one side, as if looking from a different angle might change what he saw. Carefully he removed his sunglasses and his complexion drained.

Marla spoke first, directly at Greg. 'What on earth are you up to, sneaking around and following us out here like this? Must have taken some doing, Greg Martin, but if you think this is a way to wheedle back into my life, you're mistaken.'

Stunned, Greg was slowly shaking his head. 'Marla? What are you doing here?' He looked to Roxy, who now stood behind her friend, then Nate, and finally his face filled with dark understanding. His jaw jutting forward, he slotted his sunglasses in his shirt's top pocket and glared at his friend.

'You'd better start talking,' Greg said, 'and for both our sakes, it'd better be good.'

Nate wasn't sure how he managed it, but he persuaded everyone to sit calmly around the faded cedar setting, positioned beneath the homestead's corrugated-iron verandah roof, without having his head torn off. Given the tight line of Marla's mouth, she didn't want to share space with Greg, and from the vein pulsing at Greg's temple, he wasn't too comfortable being around Nate right now. But the only alternative was grand theft auto of the Glenrowans' pickup or finding a willing kangaroo to piggyback home, so the pair held their tempers and listened.

Serenaded by bush birds and fortified by tall glasses of Mrs Glenrowan's cool lemonade, Nate explained how this situation had come about, starting with his visit to Roxy's salon. He made clear that Roxy had agreed to this plan only after Marla had announced her trip to California. He also emphasized his belief that to do nothing was sometimes worse than forging ahead with only the best intentions in mind.

He concluded, 'Marla, you're understandably hurt by those photos, and Greg had done all he thought he could to apologize and make that hurt up to you. But maybe if you both sit down and talk about it, face to face, something can be resolved, even if it's only shedding some of these bad feelings before Marla goes to California.'

When Marla quietly groaned and flicked a not entirely repulsed glance Greg's way, Nate's hopes lifted. If she was willing to at least listen, that was a start. But then she pushed to her feet, her slim nostrils flared, and she spoke to Roxy.

'I don't know if I can ever forgive you for putting me in this position.' Her eyes began to glisten. 'After everything we've been through together, you do this.'

While Roxy bowed her head, Marla went to move back inside. But then Greg stood too.

'She only did what she hoped was right,' he said. 'Hell, Marla, if we're talking about friendship, these two are the best. Roxy and Nate have faith in us. Can't you have a little faith too? Just enough to at least hear me out properly.' His heart in his eyes, he stepped forward. 'You're the person I wanted to share the rest of my life with. I still want that, more than anything.'

Nate held that breath while Roxy bit her lip and Marla

glared at her ex. Little by little, the pain in her expression morphed into something less hostile and more yielding.

'I guess I know you didn't do this to hurt me, Roxy,' Marla said. 'It's just so... Well, I never dreamed...' Gathering herself, she drew up tall. 'I suppose, given you and Nate went to all this trouble and we're here, Greg and I could talk.' When Greg sighed out a smile and tipped forward, Marla put up both her palms. 'That in no way means I've changed my mind. Only that I'm willing to hear anything new you have to say.' She looked to Roxy. 'How many days are we here?'

'Four,' Roxy said.

Hugging herself, Marla gazed out over the endless plain of red dirt, tufts of Mitchell grass, drooping eucalypts, and muttered, 'Guess I'd better unpack.'

'I thought we might go for a swim,' Nate pitched in. 'The website shows a great-looking creek nearby.'

'*If* you can believe a photo on a website.'

Marla was being wry about Greg's predicament but she had a point. That website made this place look like an Outback palace. Maybe once—a long time ago. Not that luxury was needed for love to thrive. Heck, just look at his parents.

As Marla headed back inside, Greg picked up his bag. 'I should thank you both for organizing this, but I'll hold off to see how it all pans out. I could as easily end up with a fry pan landing on my head as getting Marla's arms back around me.' He moved off. 'Hope you have something amazing lined up for your next Act.'

Sitting in that flaky timber setting, shards of early afternoon sun slanting in, Roxy had never looked more beautiful or more uncertain. She gripped her chair's arm and waited until Greg was out of earshot before asking, 'I know the overall plan but...what exactly *do* we have lined up?'

Nate leaned closer and, fighting the overwhelming urge to tell her to forget about the other two for a moment and to concentrate working on them, he assured her.

'Our next move can't fail. It involves heating things up at the same time they're both cooling down.'

She nodded slowly. 'The creek.'

'You and I can splash around, share a bit of laughter and lift this mood. When they lower their guard, join in and start talking, we'll leave them to their own devices.'

'I packed a swimsuit.'

'I'm hoping swimsuits won't be needed for long.' When she flashed him a look, he back-pedalled quick. 'For Greg and Marla, I mean.'

Suspicion darkened her face. 'I agreed to help. I'm here. But in case you have something else in mind, I'll be clear. *Not happening.*'

He feigned innocence. 'What's not happening?'

'Us getting too close.'

'How close is too close?'

She deadpanned, 'Kissing-distance close, Nate.'

'Thing is, I think if we show Marla that we've gotten over our differences, she'd be more amenable to getting over theirs.'

'Only we *haven't* gotten over our differences.'

'Right.' His gaze flicked to her full pink lips, then back to her determined gaze and he shrugged. 'I just thought you meant what you said.'

'And just what did I say?'

'That you liked me holding you.' He leaned a smidgeon closer. 'Kissing you.'

Her eyes widened and her mouth quivered before she found a threadbare voice. 'That is *not* the point.'

'What is the point?'

'That you have some crazy idea about curses and, frankly, I don't trust you.'

He remembered the way she'd moved against him, the way she'd sighed in her throat. She'd trusted him then—before she'd frozen up. Now he wondered again. 'You never did tell me why you got distracted that night on your couch.'

A blush stained her cheeks and she gripped that chair arm again. 'None of that matters now.'

'Because you believe in letting bygones be bygones?'

'Because you and me—*us, Nate*—we're done. I agreed to come here only to help Marla, not get all up-close-and-personal with you.'

She stormed inside, a clapped-out screen door slamming behind her, while Nate bit down to stop himself from hauling her back and letting her know just how wrong she was. She thought they were done? Seeing her again, having her near—it only made his reasoning these past days clearer. Stronger. Maybe he wouldn't make love to Roxy the way he'd been dreaming, but one thing was certain.

With four days and four nights, it wouldn't be for lack of trying.

CHAPTER SIX

THE creek turned out to be divine—a wide meandering stream shaded by the far-reaching branches of sleepy coolabahs. The water, babbling over a scattering of polished stones, was clearer than any Roxy had seen. Given the hot afternoon, with neither breeze nor cloud to soften the hard beat of the sun, it also looked wonderfully cool.

Cool was precisely what this scene called for.

Half an hour after Nate's confession on the verandah, Marla sat nearby atop a flat rock overhanging the water, tight-lipped and looking as if she'd rather be chewing ground glass. His face hard, Greg was throwing stones into the water, waiting for the ripples to die before casting another. From the concentrated expression on Nate's face, he was concocting a way to break the deadlock.

Roxy huffed.

Good luck with that.

Suddenly animated, Nate kicked off his shoes, then rubbed his hands together. 'Well, no use standing around. I'm going in. Who's joining me?' The other two ignored him, so he turned to Roxy and asked, 'How about it?'

She forced a smile when inside she was shaking. Not because of Marla and Greg's continuing standoff—although that was discouraging. Not because she was about to peel off this dress and reveal her figure in a bikini, even if her thighs and butt were larger than she'd have liked. What troubled her was what Nate had planned. Some splashing, he'd said. A little laughter. Together in that creek. Perhaps it wasn't too late to back out, go home.

Surveying the water, Nate began removing his shirt, absently unbuttoning, then rolling one big shoulder out of the fabric and the next while Roxy could only stare. Many times, particularly late at night, she'd imagined him sans shirt. She'd expected broad and naturally bronzed, but never this much superbly honed sinew and muscle. That body belonged on a billboard.

Then he started on his jeans.

But, hand on fly, he stilled. She felt him look over and, guilty, her gaze flew up to his. He was smiling, a smouldering knowing grin that lit his eyes and set her face and blood on fire.

Gathering her thoughts, she cleared her throat and angled away. From the corner of her eye, she saw him strolling over…felt him studying her from top to curling toe.

'You're coming in, aren't you?' He eased the jeans down over two long hard thighs. 'Need some help? A zip maybe?'

Sparks rushed through her veins. His remark was meant to remind her of that afternoon in her shop and how he'd drawn her near a heartbeat before his mouth had claimed hers. She'd been lost in his embrace that day—that night too, as well as the evening when he'd dropped her off from Marla and Greg's engagement party six months ago. Each time they'd been fully clothed. The only bare flesh had been their lips, their hands. If he touched her now, given what he *wasn't* wearing, her feet might *never* find the ground.

Jeans kicked aside, he ran a thumb around the inside band of black shorts that hung perfectly on his lean hips. Was it the trail of dark hair, or the hard outline of sculpted abdominal muscles that dipped beneath the band of shorts beside his thumb? Whatever the lure, that span between navel and what those shorts were hiding shouldn't be allowed out in public without a licence.

When she caught his words, 'Maybe I should throw you in,' Roxy was hauled back.

'Don't you dare!'

'What if I do?'

As he prowled closer, those gorgeous shoulders rolling towards her, she backed up and warned him, 'You never know. I might scream.'

'I'll risk it.'

'You don't take those kinds of risks.'

'Maybe I'm on the cusp of a change.'

'And maybe my hair is green.'

Her back met with a massive tree trunk. Boulders rose up either side. Attempt at escape was useless.

Grinning, he kept coming until his chest was so close, if she'd tipped forward a few degrees, she could run her lips over that masterpiece and taste it.

His voice lowered to a deep and private whisper. 'Hey, I think we have their attention.'

She blinked and almost asked, *Whose attention?* But then elements other than the bone-melting effect of his musky scent and body heat filtered through the fog, and she remembered the true situation and slid a surreptitious look the warring couple's way. Although pretending not to, both Marla and Greg were watching, interested, obviously waiting for their next move.

Nate whispered again, a hypnotic sexy drawl.

'Now, take off your clothes.'

Her skin flashing hot, Roxy moistened her lips. But she was overreacting. Of course, he knew she wore a swimsuit underneath. She corrected him.

'You mean take off my *dress*.'

'That's a start.' He cocked his head and summed her up again, his X-ray gaze devouring every inch.

'On second thought,' he said, 'I vote we strip you in the water.'

Knees gone to jelly, she pressed back against the trunk and tried to sound unaffected. 'Who said anything about a vote? This isn't a democracy.'

'You're right.' His brows nudged together. 'It's not.'

He moved so fast, she didn't have time to duck under his arm or try to push him away, not that either move would've made a difference. When Nate scooped her up, she was faced with a testosterone-infused power that both alarmed and, frankly, excited her too. As those muscles locked her effortlessly in and he carried her with sure long strides towards the creek, she felt energized and aroused— a glaring contrast to how she *ought* to feel. She should be outraged, not secretly plagued by the desire to press more into the hard hot feel of him. At least she was genuinely shrieking, kicking her legs and begging that he let her down. If she went swimming, she'd get in at her own pace.

Nate crashed through the water, cool wet soaked up her dress and, laughing, he asked, 'Would you rather fast or slow?'

'What are you talking about?'

'Do you prefer to be dumped or swirled in bit by bit?'

Pushing a palm against his granite chest, she struggled and muttered, 'As if my opinion counts.'

'I like the idea of hearing you scream out my name as I throw you up into the air. But drawing out the experience, taking it slow, appeals even more.'

The fiend. He wasn't talking about the water. He was letting her know how he wanted to take her in a physical, purely sexual sense, even after she'd told him again that wasn't happening. And it *wasn't*. Nothing could make her climb on that hot-cold, curse-on/curse-off, merry-go-round again, no matter how incredibly wonderful his body looked, smelled. *Felt*.

When he swirled around, pebbles crunched beneath his feet and silky water sluiced up her back, over her hips. Loathing to be dropped, she clung on, one arm twined around his strong neck. The hand that had previously pushed at him was now, of necessity, gripping one exceptionally firm pec. He checked out her hold and arched a brow.

'I think you're enjoying this.'

She growled. 'Enjoy *this*.'

Reaching down, she swept up a handful and flung water up at his face.

His every fibre seemed to tense before he shook his head quickly to shift the glistening droplets from his hair. Growling himself now—but with pleasure, not irritation—he pinned her with a devilish look that made her regret she'd tested him. His grin slowly grew, then, without warning, as she'd feared, she was dropped into the drink.

Two seconds later, she came up spluttering—and, damn the man, ready to fight.

She jumped at him—*on* him—and somehow managed to push him over. Or had he simply let her? Either way, she was on top now and intended to take every advantage. Pushing on his shoulders, she forced his smirk under the ripples. The next instant, he was pushing back, jettisoning her over and into the stream.

She battled back and he let her gain ground before he secured her—his hands around and near spanning her waist—while she thrashed and twisted. She'd never been more riled...and he'd never seemed more attractive, particularly with his chest filled with rumbling laughter.

Thing was that she was laughing too—and so hard, she felt *filled* with it.

As the moment stretched out the struggling and laughter eased, but they continued holding and steadying each other. Her hands at the base of his neck, his clasped around her middle, their laboured breathing evened as Roxy grew profoundly aware of those male fingers digging into her flesh, of the way his gaze stroked her lips and how desperately she wanted him to act again without asking permission. This minute. *Now.* She needed him to go ahead and kiss her till the world stopped turning and she couldn't remember who she was, or where, or why...

Without conscious thought, her fingers filed up the cool wet column of his throat, over the hot pulse that beat below his ear, then around the sexy sandpaper-rough of his jaw while his loaded gaze smouldered into hers. As her heartbeat thundered on she drew a line along the bow of his full lower lip and marvelled at how his expression intensified and the muscles in her belly contracted and warmed.

With painstaking care, he lifted her a little higher so that her still-sandalled toes left the creek floor. Falling deeper into the trance, she allowed her eyes to drift shut while she waited for their lips to touch...for his mouth to capture and consume her. Instead she heard her name murmured as if the words had come from afar.

'Roxy, it's over.'

Her eyes dragged open. His face—that mouth—was tantalizingly close and his breath was teasingly warm on her cheek. Wasn't this what he wanted? Why on earth was he waiting?

'What's over?' she asked.

'They've gone. Or at least I'm pretty sure they are.'

Her first thought was to bat those words aside. All she cared about was melding into Nate's caress, knowing more about this sizzle and pull. But as he continued to look down at her, dark brows knitted, her mind shifted and she swam up from the haze. The splashing, joking—*flirting…*

This wasn't for *their* benefit. It was for Marla and Greg's.

If she'd thought her heart had hammered before, this moment her chest—her entire body—felt as if it were booming. Nate's charm never failed to entice her. *Entrap* her. She was as vulnerable this moment as she'd been every other time they'd touched. Her nerve-endings buzzing, she felt aroused to her very core.

But more so she was embarrassed. He'd told her they should let their friends believe they'd got past their differences. But Greg and Marla weren't the only ones fooled. And why shouldn't she be convinced? Nate should give lessons.

Water dripping down her face, she angled to see. Where previously their friends had stood, only dry gum leaves now lay. Lowering her arms, she flicked her wet hands and assumed a resigned mask.

'Maybe they've gone for a trek down the bank.'

Mr Glenrowan had suggested they take his pickup in case, after a big swim, anyone was too tired to walk back. Parking just beyond the bank's skirt of trees, Nate had left the keys in the ignition. Now, they heard that engine splutter to life. Next came a series of distant gear crunches, then the sound of tyres rolling away.

Roxy slouched. 'Well, that was a waste of time.'

'Depends how you look at it.'

The smile and intent was back in his eyes. A pulse popped low in his cheek at the same time his attention dipped to sweep a scorching line across her lips. Then he tipped closer, edged damp hair aside and dropped a light moist kiss on a particularly sensitive part of her neck.

'I don't think they'll come back,' he murmured. 'Doesn't mean we have to leave.' He nuzzled along the line of her jaw, then, at last, his mouth veered towards hers and brushed a single haunting time.

Their lips all but touching, they peered into each other's eyes. When his head drew back an inch, caught again in the tide, she followed and this time her lips did the grazing—once, twice and over again. He might drive her mad but, this minute, she had less than no willpower where he was concerned. If he didn't kiss her in earnest and soon, to hell with it. She'd latch on and drag his head down herself.

Instead, his hot palms slid up over the front of her dress and she began to dissolve as he took his time releasing each button. With drops running down her back, her arms, and her mind and senses racing, she stood before him quivering, waiting, until finally the dress fell into the water that ringed her thighs. Reaching around, he undid her bikini top and caught the scrap of yellow Lycra before it dropped. Then one palm sculpted over the bare-skinned curve of her waist, a hip, at the same time he carefully hunkered down.

While she held her breath, he released her bikini bottom bows then two long fingers slid between her legs and dragged the wet bottoms out. He bunched them in the same hand that held the top, curled his free palm around her back upper thigh and urged her forward when his head slanted and came in.

His mouth touched her just shy of her sex and when the stiff tip of his tongue tickled the spot, her neck rocked back and hands automatically fisted in the damp of his hair. Despite the cool water, she burned all over. Her blood felt on fire and her lungs couldn't grasp enough air. Then he was sucking, so lightly, with such skill, Roxy worried she might begin to shake beneath the thrill of it. He shifted slightly and, the next she knew, his scratchy chin was rubbing up the sensitive cleft at the apex of her thighs.

Flames shot through her body. She didn't care that they were out in the open. Hell, she wouldn't have the strength to stop if they were making love in the centre of Sydney. And standing here completely naked, enjoying the waves he so effortlessly whipped up inside her, she only wanted the sensations—the way he played and moved with her— to go on and on.

His head came down enough for his lips to nuzzle then to stroke her with his tongue. She clenched—her thighs, her stomach, her teeth—and ploughed her fingers over the back of his scalp, across that broad slick ledge of shoulder. His hand bracing the back of her thigh, he pressed her in more and hummed in satisfaction as he drew that small pulsing part of her into his mouth.

A thousand tingling darts lit and, within minutes, had joined to hover, ready to rush in and explode all at once. But then the stroking eased and half of her breathless tension drained away. In another world, she swayed as he eased to his feet, his chest sliding against her until they again stood face to face. Before she could focus, his mouth crashed down, taking hers in a way that had her wondering if this was the same man.

Starving. Single-minded.

Committed.

His mouth covering hers, he collected her in his arms and moved to the edge of the creek where he laid her upon the soft grass-covered bank, then straightened to stand before her. Water rushed down his glistening chest, packed abs, powerful arms. Then the shorts came off and she couldn't drag her eyes away. He was tall and built, but like never before she realized Nate Sparks was a strong man—and a fully aroused one. As he lowered over her his hard heat ironed down her front until his mouth found the sensitive tip of her breast.

Each in turn, he teased her nipples, alternatively twirling his tongue and nipping the beads while his hand took over what his mouth had taken such pleasure in only moments before. The spiral of sensation was immediate and so fierce, she could feel the promise of release a mere breath away. Being with Nate this way felt so extraordinary, so altogether new, and yet on a different plane, she wondered if in another life they'd met like this before.

His jeans had landed nearby. Light-headed, she realized he was wrestling with the belt—no, the pocket—and drawing something out. A foil wrap. Protection. But when he shifted up to sheath himself, needing to measure and pleasure him, she caught him in one hand, squeezed and led him back. Groaning out a shuddering sigh, he gradually lowered back down and, curving an arm around her head, tenderly kissed her again.

Lying in the dappled sunshine, she worked his length from base to tip and down again, revelling in the way he moved with her while his throat made gravelled, grateful sounds. When he'd hardened to steel and she sensed his dam about to break, reluctantly she pulled back and let him see to the condom.

A heartbeat later, he was hovering above her, reaching around to find her calf and bring that leg over the back of his own steely thigh. Her every cell sizzling, Roxy ran her fingers through the wiry hair on his chest and gazed into hooded blue eyes that she knew at this minute saw only her.

'I couldn't have spent my life not knowing this,' he said, 'not know you like this. I wouldn't have let you go.'

When he entered her, she was beyond ready, and yet that initial nudge caught her breath. As a lit-fuse of sensation ripped through her his head dropped into her drying hair and he murmured more words that brought happy tears to her eyes. Then he began to move, a powerful yet measured rhythm that matched the deep steady beating of her heart.

Soon the ache of need was everywhere—her *everything*. While the burn at her core continued to condense and glow, each second a little stronger, a little brighter, he hitched up so that his elbows were locked and embedded in the grass either side of her shoulders. His hands clasped hers where they'd fallen over her head and as their fingers twined he closed his eyes and lifted his face, inch by inch, towards the sun. When he moved again, driving in deeper, thrusting harder, he struck a spot so unstable, so combustible, she groaned deep in her throat and, on reflex, pressed in around him.

A barely contained fire began to crackle and leap at the same instant Roxy found herself suspended high above the world with only a glimmer of all things perfect to keep her from falling. As if they'd reached the same plateau at the exact same moment, Nate took breath and stilled too. A line of perspiration running from the corner of his brow, he put strain aside long enough to smile into her eyes, then slowly, carefully, he moved again.

A moment later, on first a tremor, then a gasp, she was thrown towards the stars and shattered into a million fiery pieces.

CHAPTER SEVEN

'You're wondering, aren't you?'

The surrounding eucalypts' minty smell had softened as the day's heat had waned and Nate couldn't remember a time when he'd felt more at peace. But now, hearing Roxy's drowsy question, he slipped from beneath the blanket of his post-coital buzz and absorbed more the amazing reality of what had just transpired. Her cheek resting on his chest, he stroked her hair as they lay twined together among the reeds lining the Glenrowan Homestead creek.

Roxy Trammel was fierce and beautiful and sexy and *fun*. Play-fighting in the water, kissing him near senseless on this bank… Nate only wished he could put life and its complications on hold long enough to enjoy more than four days soaking up this unique kind of joy.

Eyes closing again, he feathered his lips over the damp dome of her crown, breathed in the fresh-water scent clinging to her hair and wound his mind back to her question. She thought he was wondering about something?

In a low gravelled voice, he said, 'Only about having you again.'

When his nether regions jerked at the thought, he mustered his energy, pushed up and slid back into the water, dragging Roxy and her delectable curves along with him. Mid-stream, he wrapped her purposefully in his arms and, while she smiled and ironed herself up against him, he dropped meaningful kisses upon her shoulder, over the honeyed slope of her throat.

'Actually,' she murmured, tracing her nails along his nape and making him groan with want, 'I wondered if you might think I was sorry this happened.'

His heartbeat and nuzzling stopped. 'Are you?'

'Yes.' His head snapped up. 'And no,' she finished and lifted one brow. 'I was determined not to let you get close.'

'Well, you can't get much closer than this. Although I'd like to try.' He drew a lazy circle around that adorable dimple in her cheek. 'Guess this was always going to happen.'

'So, now that it's out of our systems—'

'It's not out of mine.'

That dimple deepened as her eyes darkened. 'It was good, wasn't it?'

'Not good.' His lips skimmed her brow. 'It was great.'

Over the next few minutes, he discovered new places to explore, highly sensitive spots that drove up her breathing and left the skin on her arms covered in tiny bumps. As her fingers fanned over his chest, stopping every so often to circle and pluck a small flat disc, his erection grew and grew. On autopilot, he bent at the knees, got a good grip on her flanks, then hoisted her up. The tips of her breasts tickling his collarbones, she wrapped her legs around his hips, her arms around his neck, and curled in as he manoeuvred her lower half, pleasing and teasing them both. When his tip then entire shaft filled her once again, she sucked back a breath and melted against him.

By the time he remembered protection, Roxy looked to be enjoying the action more than he was, if that was possible. Her fingers digging into his shoulders, her neck rocked back while she drove him on; Nate had to lock his every thought and fibre to maintain control. He was that close to letting go.

Her head coming forward, her lips brushing his, she murmured in a thick creamy voice, 'Shouldn't we see what's happened to our friends?'

He kissed the hollow of her throat, her chin, her swollen parted lips. 'Soon.'

'They might think we drowned.'

'In the most pleasurable way possible.'

Biting down, he pushed in to the hilt and Roxy caught her breath, stilled then, releasing a quivering sigh, began to move again.

After a few more minutes, when his legs had begun to shake from the strain of holding back the tide, she said, 'I thought our mission was to get those two back together, not to—'

Her breathless enunciation of that four-letter word was the most erotic thing he'd ever heard. If he didn't stop now, it would be too late. He disengaged those vital mindless parts even as he kept her close. He needed a second condom and he needed it now.

'They could be off talking somewhere,' he replied, moving with her towards the bank and thinking, *Not that I want to talk at this precise moment.*

'Or they could be organizing separate lifts out of this place.'

Drawing back, he examined her furrowed brow. Roxy might have surrendered to the friction sparking between them, but now her pendulum had swung back to helping her friend. His rational mind said she was right. They should get back. But his sexually activated thought patterns were demanding more time alone. What difference would ten minutes make?

When her chin tucked in and she frowned, Nate realized he'd spoken that last aloud. Determined now, Roxy wiggled away and tramped onto the bank.

'After ignoring her like that, I wouldn't be surprised if Marla refused to talk to me again.'

'You weren't ignoring her. We were setting the mood. But you're right,' he conceded. 'We'll need to work harder if we want to move this forward.'

Her back to him, he let his gaze savour a most tempting rear view as she retied her bikini bottoms then top. Dragging a hand over his chest, already missing her warmth, he waded out too.

She found her dress. 'Moving forward means making sure they spend time together.'

'And that they see firsthand how fences are mended—' coming up behind, he traced his cheek gently up hers '—and how good making up can be.'

She threw an uncertain look over her shoulder. 'As long as we don't get too distracted.'

'I've been nothing *but* distracted.' He edged her around and, setting his forehead to hers, confessed, 'Since that night you kicked me out, I haven't stopped thinking about you.'

She recoiled. 'Please tell me you're not going to mention that curse again.'

'I'm not going to mention that curse again.'

'No more talk about underachieving or not measuring up to all that you can be?'

Casting aside a mental snapshot of Roxy in that white wedding gown, of his business plan going down the gurgler, he nodded. 'Promise.'

And, if he could say that and mean it, couldn't he lighten up more and invite Roxy to his parents' anniversary bash? His folks could conjecture and lean all they pleased. How far a relationship went was up to him. He certainly enjoyed

making love to Roxy, more than any woman he'd been
with, but he still had all his faculties, didn't he? Hadn't
been blinded by a supernova flash of everlasting love and
the overwhelming urge to propose and throw his career
away. In fact, he felt bolstered. Strong.

Hell, he felt fan-freakin'-*tastic*!

Clearing his throat, Nate got ready to mention that his
parents had been married thirty-one years, which would
lead to a comment about the party and fact that he'd like
her to accompany him, when, looking past his shoulder,
Roxy yelped, laughed, then slapped a hand over her mouth
as if wanting to take the noise back.

'Did you see that?'

Her finger shook at a place in the creek where ripples had spread out from a central point. Nate glimpsed
a shadow wriggling beneath the water's surface…a fur-
covered animal with a bill for a beak. She gripped his
shoulder with both hands and whispered, 'A platypus. I
wonder if she has a nest? They really do look like a cross
between a beaver and a duck. So cute!'

'They have spurs on their back paws.' Frowning, he
looked around for a stick or a rock. 'I think there might
be poison involved.'

Certainly they could have fun, but reality was they were
in the wild here, not a suburban backyard.

Roxy only laughed. 'Okay, Worry Wart. We won't disturb her.'

Turning, he slid his palm up her slender waist, over
those beautiful buoyant breasts. Memories of the snug feel
of her, the fresh feminine taste, filled his mind and, slipping into the zone again, he brought her gorgeous body
close.

But, with a grin and shake of her head, she wound away
and headed for the path out. Beaten, he slapped his hands

against his thighs, then slipped into his shoes, slung his jeans and shirt over one shoulder and, jogging to catch up, followed her out.

'Guess we should leave before a bunyip gets you,' he said, fitting his hat.

'Why me? Why not *us*?'

'They only like the flesh of women.' Securing her hand in his, he helped her through orchid-tipped sprays of emu bush and out onto the open plain. 'Aboriginal folklore says they lurk around creeks and billabongs.'

'I read somewhere they look like gargoyles.'

'Some say they resemble snarling dogs with flippers. Or are covered in feathers with tails like a horse.'

'You really do have an imagination.'

'Says the woman who creates bunny wedding gowns.'

His arm sliding around her waist, still damp and cool from their swim, he inhaled air that dried his throat in two minutes flat. The Glenrowan Homestead was a smudge of grey paint on the horizon. Plenty of time to bring up that other issue.

'My parents are throwing a party this weekend,' he said. 'An annual event.'

'Their anniversary?'

However did she guess? 'I wondered if you'd like to go.' He expected curiosity. Maybe a spark of interest. Instead she nibbled her lip and averted her gaze. His chuckle was hollow. 'Don't act so excited.'

She wound hair behind her ear. 'Are you sure you want me to go?'

'I asked, didn't I?'

'Let's see how you feel when we get home.'

His eyebrows hiked up. 'You think I'll change my mind?'

'I don't think it's a good idea to rush into anything.'

'It's an invitation to a party, not to share the rest of our lives together.' When she nibbled again, he smiled crookedly. 'I'm breaking through my barriers. It's a good thing.'

'I'm not so sure—'

'Well, I am.' He blinked, then cocked his head as a thought struck. 'Or is this hedging about you?'

'Me?'

Walking on, he shrugged. 'Maybe you have more of a hang-up than I do.'

'I doubt that's possible.'

'Did you see your dad much after he left?'

'What has that got to do with—?'

But as her words cut off and the defensive glint in her eyes faded, she let out a breath and started walking again. He wasn't poking fun at her, merely making a point. If he'd had a family background reason for wanting to stay clear of 'trouble', well, so did she.

'After he married again, my mother insisted I visit every other weekend,' she began. 'She said he and I both deserved to know one another. Now I wonder if she sent me to get information more than anything. But his second wife didn't like me much, which was fine because I didn't much like her either. My visits dwindled off to hardly ever. When that marriage broke up too, I began to visit again. Until I found new perfume bottles stashed under the bathroom sink and different nightdresses peeking out from under my father's pillow. He married that third time and I honestly hoped he'd found the one.' Her mouth tightened. 'As far as my father is concerned, one woman was never enough.'

'Do you talk to him now?'

'I guess. I can't forget that he hurt us, but I've tried to, you know…forgive.' With the afternoon sun casting longer shadows over the parched red ground, she grunted. 'I told him once how much he'd hurt me, but he didn't understand. He said he'd never stopped loving me. I don't think he knows what love is.'

'Was he a good dad in other ways?'

'When I was very young, I remember him kissing my forehead every night before I fell asleep. He'd tell me I was his special princess. Growing up, I had these two totally different ideas of him clashing around in my head. There was even a part of me that understood why my mother didn't want to confront him over his extramarital affairs and possibly have him leave.' Her guilty gaze shot across to him. 'I've never admitted that to anyone.'

'You wanted your father. I understand completely.'

A small smile touched her lips, her eyes.

'He could be a whole lot of fun,' she explained. 'A charmer.' She sent a wry look. 'A little like you.'

'Trust me.' He tugged her closer. 'He's nothing like me.'

'My great-aunt Leasie got caught up with a charmer once,' she went on, matching her steps with his. 'Harry Mercer. He made a living selling bogus life assurance in the sixties. She dropped him cold when she found out. He still writes to her from prison, but she never responds. Sometimes I think she'd like to, but she's too smart to bend, even a little.'

'Did your aunt ever marry?'

'She's happy alone.' Roxy corrected herself. 'That's not entirely true. She collects budgerigars. Small. Friendly. Low maintenance.'

'Unlike men.'

'Unlike men like Harry.'

Or like her philandering father. Nate might try to manipulate a situation to get the best outcome for all concerned, but no one could ever accuse him of being disloyal. He might not want to rush down any aisle but when he married, it would be in every sense 'for ever'. Why do something if you didn't intend to do it properly?

As they entered the homestead's yard through the dilapidated picket fence Nate lifted his nose to the air. 'I smell bread baking.'

'This is the bush. Bet it's damper.' Australia's iconic soda bread traditionally baked over the coals of a fire.

Nate sniffed again. 'And some kind of stew.' He held his growling stomach. He hadn't eaten since soggy sandwiches on the plane.

A distant curlew called—a hauntingly lonely sound, Nate thought—and to one side of the homestead's steps, Mr Glenrowan tended a campfire. Suspended over the low-licking flames hung two Bedourie ovens—the Outback's steel-modelled version of the cast-iron Dutch oven. One oven for the stew, Nate guessed. One for the damper.

Looking up, Mr Glenrowan grinned and pushed to his feet. 'I wondered when you two would show up. Your friends've been back a while.'

Roxy's cheeks went pink, and not from the sun. 'Where are they now?'

'Marla's in helping the wife.'

'And I've been collecting wood for the fire.'

Nate searched out that familiar second male voice. Greg was rounding the homestead's corner, a bundle in his arms.

Mr Glenrowan nodded at Greg's stash. 'Good work. Set 'em down there.' He moved towards the steps. 'I'll go see what's keeping those girls.'

Obviously eager to touch base with Marla, Roxy hurried after him. 'I'll go too.'

His expression wry, Greg stopped before his friend. 'All cooled off now?'

Nate removed his hat and pulled on his shirt. 'You should've come in for a swim.'

'Haven't you heard? Three's a crowd.'

'You're forgetting Marla.'

'No. Marla's forgotten me.' Greg set the wood down and stayed crouched beside the fire, watching the flames. 'When you and Roxy got involved, she headed off. I followed. We took the pickup back here. Hell, we even talked.'

'Greg, that's great!'

'About an uncle of hers who owned a property. She explained at length how he'd castrate young bulls. Apparently they'll break through any paddock to get to a cow in heat. She even described the tool used.' Greg visibly shuddered. 'By the time I turned off that rickety old engine, I felt nauseous.'

Nate winced but pointed out, 'She's testing you.'

'Tell my testicles that.'

Nate flicked a look at the verandah. 'She'll be out soon and you'll have another chance. Just follow my lead. Loosen up.'

Greg stopped poking a stick at the flames to peer up. 'What is it with you two anyway? I thought you weren't interested in seeing Roxy again.' One thick brow arched. 'I'm guessing you saw plenty of each other in that creek.'

After that engagement party where he and Roxy had obviously hit it off, Nate had only ever mentioned that he hadn't wanted to see her again. That she seemed highly strung and didn't want to see him again either. He guessed Roxy had told Marla a similar story to suit. No use bringing up kisses and curses. Greg would only laugh and harder than Roxy had. So now Nate told his friend the truth—or a good portion of it.

'Me and Roxy together, here…well, it's an act.'

'An act for what?'

'To show Marla that people deserve a second chance.'

'What I saw happening in that creek between you two was no act.'

'We were mucking around. Hell, I'm a man, she's a woman—'

'And if water hadn't been involved, the flames would've been hotter than these.' He tossed the stick into glowing ashes. 'A crowbar couldn't have pried you two apart.'

'Which only goes to show. If Roxy and I can move forward, imagine how easy it'd be if you got close to Marla for a few minutes.'

Thinking that through, Greg scratched his temple and gradually found his feet. 'Maybe, if I had the right mood, the right opportunity…'

'Roxy and I can help with the first. Then it's up to you.' That screen door squeaked open, slapped shut. He sent Greg a private wink. 'Follow my lead.'

Carrying a bowl of salad, Roxy headed down the stairs. Next came Mr Glenrowan with plates. His wife and Marla followed with napkins, condiments and cutlery.

Mr Glenrowan saw to the damper and laid the bread in the centre of a wobbly outdoor table. 'Butter's there if you want it.'

Nate pulled a piece off the incredibly fresh, steamy loaf and sank his teeth in. Lord, he was famished. But then he remembered Roxy, his manners and the plan. Setting down the bread, he dusted his hands and asked, 'Can I cut you a slice?'

She nodded. 'With a dollop of butter on the side.'

After Nate was finished, Greg came forward, sliced off two pieces and brought one to Marla.

'No butter,' he said. 'Right?'

Marla's eyes widened as if she were taken aback or alarmed by his civility, but then she accepted the plate, even offered a small smile.

Seeing to the second pot, Mr Glenrowan lifted the lid and stirred the contents until a hearty aroma drifted into Nate's lungs and taste buds began to water.

'On a guest's first night,' Mr Glenrowan said, slipping the pot's handle off its rod with the help of a folded tea towel, 'we always eat under the stars.' He surveyed the sky, which had succumbed to a far-reaching dusk, then put the pot on the table. 'Grab some stew and go pull up a log.'

He indicated three log-cum-benches positioned in a U around the fire. After filling their plates with beef and bean stew, Nate and Roxy took the log nearest the homestead. Greg sat on the second of three. Marla took the third.

Roxy set a spoonful of stew to her mouth then, wincing, pulled it quickly away. 'It's hot.'

'Let some steam escape.' Nate took her spoon and wound the utensil back and forth through the stew for a moment or two. Then he lifted a spoonful and asked, 'Mind if I test it?'

Amused, Roxy shrugged. 'Sure. Go ahead.'

Nate set the spoon to his upper lip, smiled and handed it over. 'Should be fine now.'

He wouldn't offer to cool just anyone's dinner but in truth he was only repeating what he'd done many times for the younger kids growing up. Still, it occurred to him now that Greg was eyeing Marla's plate, maybe wondering if her stew was too hot. But she wasn't giving him a chance to help if it was. Dunking her damper, she sopped up stew juice before taking a big, 'I'm fine without you' bite.

Obviously feeling the ripple of unease, Roxy started a conversation. 'Nate and I were talking about bunyips.'

Chuckling, Mr Glenrowan made himself comfortable on Greg's log. 'Noisy beasts.'

Marla swallowed and slanted her head. 'You believe in monsters?'

'Out here,' Mrs Glenrowan said, sitting herself along-side Marla, 'you get to believe in all kinds of things.'

Mr Glenrowan stirred his stew. 'It's actually owls that nest near creeks that make those terrible screeching noises—like a woman's scream.'

Marla lowered her damper slice. 'Are they nesting at the moment?'

'You hear 'em from time to time.'

When Greg crossed to the table to grab a napkin, Mr Glenrowan crooked his finger at his wife and she moved to sit alongside him. More than willing to play musical logs, Greg didn't waste time. He sat down an arm's length away from Marla.

Pleased with the progress, Nate kept the conversation going. 'Bet there's some good ghost stories around these parts.'

'All manner of 'em,' Mr Glenrowan said.

'What's your favourite?' Roxy asked at the same time Nate caught Greg's eye and, in demonstration, sidled a little closer to her. At that moment, Marla dropped her spoon. Greg snatched it up mid-air and edged closer as he handed it back.

'We could tell them about that woman fifty years ago,' Mrs Glenrowan said, looking around the circle while the fire leapt and crackled. 'The daughter of a general on holi-day out here from America got hopelessly lost in the bush. The general and his wife spent days searching. They fi-nally found her by a creek.'

'*That* creek?' Roxy asked.

'Yes, but a ways upstream from here.'

Marla sat, riveted. 'Was she...alive?'

'She was breathing but wringing wet and stuck in a trancelike state. She kept saying the water spirit had saved her. She described a handsome man with skin dark as ebony, transparent teeth and eyes like glowing coals set way back in his skull. Every night after that, the girl wandered down to the water to wait for his return.'

In the dancing firelight, Marla's eyes grew wider. 'A ghost.'

'And her lover,' Mrs Glenrowan said. 'Nine months on, she had a baby. Same complexion as hers but the eyes...' As Mrs Glenrowan leaned forward Marla shrank towards Greg. 'The eyes were unusually bright. The same colour as the sun at midday when the sky is filled with wind and dust.'

When Marla shivered, Greg stepped in. 'Can I get you a wrap?'

Marla blinked over and found a weak smile. 'I love ghost stories but...'

'They give you bad dreams,' Greg finished for her a second before a screech echoed through the shadows and Marla jumped, landing even closer to Greg.

'It's an owl,' Mr Glenrowan said, balancing his plate on his lap while he pulled damper apart and, a knowing smile on her lips, his wife kept eating.

Nate sat back. What an intriguing couple.

'How did you two meet?' he asked.

Mrs Glenrowan—'My sister dated his brother.'

Roxy—'Did you have a double wedding?'

Nate threw in, 'Roxy designs wedding gowns,' then spotted Marla's gaze sliding Greg's way. She was thinking about wearing that gown. Thinking about the man she loved being so close. Close enough to forgive.

Mrs Glenrowan lowered her plate. 'Sadly those two didn't marry. They had an argument. A misunderstanding, really. She went off in a huff.'

'And they never made up.' Nate exhaled. For this exercise's sake, he'd hoped for a happy ending.

'Ended up she got hitched to a widower with six kids,' said Mr Glenrowan.

His wife added, 'My sister couldn't have children.'

'So it turned out for the best?' Marla asked.

'My brother never married. Still pines for her to this day.' Mr Glenrowan held his wife's hand, brought her fingers to his lips and murmured, 'I've always been the lucky one.'

'Not that we haven't had disagreements,' Mrs G pointed out.

'But you always forgive me.'

The older pair peered into each other's eyes for a long moment before Mrs Glenrowan brought herself back and let slip a coy laugh. 'Suppose I ought to see to the dishes.'

Marla stood. 'I'll do that.'

Greg stood too. 'I'll help.'

While Marla seemed to hold her breath, Nate also pushed to his feet. 'Roxy and I'll tidy up out here.'

Marla's focus went to Mrs Glenrowan, who was dabbing her napkin against a corner of her husband's mouth before lightly kissing the spot. Marla's lips swung to one side, her brow creased, then she finally nodded. She took Greg's plate first, then, collecting everyone else's in turn, moved inside.

Greg collected the damper and said to Nate, 'See you all later.'

Nate crossed mental fingers.

Hopefully much later.

The Glenrowans went for a long walk, leaving just Roxy and Nate to talk in hushed tones about the progress Greg and Marla seemed to have made this evening. For the first time since agreeing to this plot, Roxy felt truly optimistic. Maybe Nate's plan would work after all.

When the fire died and it became obvious their friends wouldn't be rejoining them, Roxy let Nate take her hand to lead her inside. As they moved up those worn wooden steps a clutch of nerves jumped in Roxy's stomach. She still glowed after their mind-blowing romp in the creek. She couldn't deny she looked forward to enjoying something similar behind closed doors tonight.

But with Greg and Marla's relationship so damaged, she also felt guilty. Hopefully those two had stuck it out during kitchen duties and were on their way to working something longer-term out. So why not enjoy a little more of what Nate had to offer? Roxy thought as they entered the house, which smelled of old wool and fresh billy tea. It wasn't as if this tryst would go on indefinitely, for more reasons than one. Although she did wonder how, and when, it would fold. Not until after that anniversary party…*if* she accepted his invitation. And, frankly, she was curious. Their Glenrowan hosts seemed completely devoted to one another. How would Nate's besotted parents compare?

How would his family welcome her?

Careful to be quiet and not disturb, they padded down a long high-ceilinged hallway walled in faded blue tongue-and-groove. At the hallway's end, they turned left and found their luggage waiting outside two separate bedroom doorways. Nate stuck his nose in one room, the other, then collected both cases and entered the first.

'This room looks like ours.'

Secretly liking the way he took charge, Roxy flicked on the light and crossed to the centre of the room. The bed was big and covered in clean comforters and pillows. An old-fashioned cedar dresser sat bumped up against the far wall. Flimsy curtains floated on the opened window's refreshing evening breeze.

She inhaled and sighed. 'It smells like rose petals in here.'

Nate flicked on a lamp, thumbed off the main light then joined her. As his hot palms curved over her hips she tipped closer, enough for their lips to almost touch. But when his head angled and his grip tightened, she wove her mouth away from his.

'You're being presumptuous.'

A knuckle on her chin turned her gaze back to his. 'Given all that talk about ghosts, I thought you could use some company tonight.'

'I'm not the nail-biting type, remember?'

Irresistibly close, his lazy grin spread. 'Then maybe you should humour me.'

Helpless to resist, she fanned her palms up beneath his shirt, over his flat stomach and relished the way his glittering blue eyes drifted shut. 'What would this humouring involve?'

'I should think lots of petting.'

Petting. 'That's an interesting term.'

'Interspersed with plenty of kissing.'

Holding his jaw with both hands, she brought her mouth to his and kissed him slow and deep and long. Finally she drew away.

'Like that?' she asked.

He growled and pulled her back. '*Just* like that.'

He kissed her even more thoroughly, ironing his palms over her hips, pressing her against him so there could be no misunderstanding about how much he wanted her. Running her fingers up his front, she began unbuttoning his shirt, but not nearly fast enough. He flicked open one button but she held his hand to stop him.

'Hey, cowboy, this is my job.'

His voice was a husky rasp. 'Just thought I'd help.'

She pretended to think it over.

'Well, okay.'

He grabbed the front tails and tore the shirt off over his head. 'There. Done.'

The shorts came off, her dress. Then he threw her over his shoulder and strode to the bed with her yelp of surprise echoing through the room. When he dropped her on the airy mattress and, one knee on the bed, hovered above her, Roxy's every cell flashed hot. With his bright eyes unusually dark, he lowered down. His arm curled possessively around her head then, as a distant curlew cried through the night, he kissed her with more hunger and need than she'd ever dreamed could be possible.

CHAPTER EIGHT

A MASCULINE groan rumbling from beneath the daisy-print covers dragged Roxy from her dreams.

Blinking open her eyes, she smiled at the morning sunshine filling the large room, then smiled all the more as memories of that incredible 'night before' tumbled through her mind. Turning her head, she assessed the rounded shape that spanned the length of the cosy double bed, the handsome face cradled deep in the feather-down pillow. She had to bite her lip to contain the sigh. She'd actually done it…got over her angst and had sex with Nate Sparks, and in several highly orgasmic ways.

The time spent at that creek yesterday afternoon was something for the textbook. Her blood smouldered to even think of the way Nate had used his hands, his voice. His tongue. And then, last night, when they'd made love again, the fireworks had exploded higher. Brighter. She couldn't believe that two people coming together could feel so much like…*magic*.

Although, when she'd curled up into his strong heat in this bed to finally fall asleep, Roxy had had a disturbing thought. If this got any better, she definitely wouldn't be able to see him again. Already he was addictive. She didn't want to get hooked, and neither would he.

She was enjoying the toasty tickly feeling in her tummy

that came from merely being with him when his hawk-ish nose wrinkled and one long impossibly toned arm stretched high. When that limb dropped over her waist, the impact whooshed air from her lungs. Still asleep, he hauled her near. Naked beneath the covers, Roxy got her breath and slid up against his hard heat. The days might get hot out here in the Outback, but early mornings were perfectly mild.

For a long satisfying time, she studied the planes and angles of his face at the same time her fingers itched to riffle through the crisp hair on his chest then filter over the slow-pulsing hollow at the base of his tanned throat. Pressed up close, Roxy indulged her memories—and fantasies—until she was aching for him to wake so they could make love again.

Maybe a friendly nudge…

Lightly she laid a bent knee over his thigh. When he muttered something, but then drifted off again, she pressed into him more and pinpricks of warmth and desire erupted all over her.

He was hard. So thick and rigid that fighting the tempta-tion to kiss and stroke him awake had become a real chal-lenge. Then he rolled towards her more and his erection poked her belly. He might not know it, but he was begging for her attentions.

With a feathery touch, she trailed a hand down over his hip, across the breadth of that steely thigh then gently—but deftly—she coiled her fingers around him and squeezed just enough.

His engorged length jerked, and again. Leaning in, she dropped a soft teasing kiss on his chest. The wiry black hair tickled her nose at the same time his musky scent drifted deep into her lungs, through her stimulated sys-tem. Still, his eyes stayed shut.

She frowned. What would it take to wake him? Maybe she should nibble his ear or trace the tip of her tongue over the seam of his lips or—

A wicked grin curved her mouth.

Or maybe I should really give him something to dream about.

With infinite care, she shifted and began to slow kiss her way down over his chest, the steely ruts of his abdomen. Her tongue wound leisurely around his navel before travelling further south until her lips grazed the hot rounded tip of his erection.

In semi-darkness beneath the covers, she took him inside her mouth and instantly her insides began to pulse. Her grip tightened a fraction as she traced her way further down, while her hold on him dragged slowly up. Her breasts rubbing against his legs, she gave herself over to the heat humming through her veins, and the kindling sparking between her own thighs.

Soon he was moving too—with her, against her. Roxy would have grinned if she'd been able. He was awake, or as awake as he needed to be.

When his movements grew to a pace and thrust she couldn't accommodate, reluctantly she released him and slid up his front, leaving a trail of burning kisses along the way. And as her face met his, she was greeted by the world's sleepiest, sexiest lopsided smile. Easing out a happy growl, he ran a palm over her crown.

'Well, this *is* a good morning.'

'I didn't think you'd ever wake up.'

'Who said I wasn't awake?'

'You were playing possum? That's not fair.'

'Way I see it, it's you who took complete advantage of me. And don't let me stop you.' Offering himself, he lay flat on his back, hands cradling his head. 'Be gentle.'

She was certain her eyes laughed even as her lips pursed to contain the smile. 'And if I'm not in the mood for gentle?'

Without warning, he flung back the covers, scooped her up and swung her over so that she straddled his lap. After a yelp of surprise, her laughter spilled out.

Grinding her hips down while he ground up, he pretended to scold her. '*Shh*. You'll wake up the house.'

'I'm not sure we didn't keep them awake last night.'

His palm fanned over one breast, the ridges of his fingers teasing and rubbing a beaded nipple. And as he moved beneath her and Roxy listened to the visceral tune playing deep inside her she found her eyes drifting shut and the pleasure begin to climb.

With a firm hold on her hips, he manoeuvred his loins and slowly entered her. A hypnotic veil fell and, without conscious thought, she began to move as time wound down to a sweet syrupy slow. Her body was everywhere, exquisite sensations her everything, and as the room grew warmer and his controlled thrusts drove deeper, almost too soon, she found herself balanced on the edge of that wonderful sparkling precipice.

For a pulse-pounding moment, she stilled, arching her spine more, needing to concentrate to maintain the sizzling status quo; this fine line between infinite understanding and heaven was just too good to let go. But as she swayed and clutched his sides her core squeezed more and the world dropped further away.

On a different plane, she recognized a comforting warmth cup her cheek and, buzzing all over, she opened heavy-lidded eyes. The sexiest, most considerate lover ever born was gazing up at her with an expression so focused and pure, it took even more of her breath away.

Perhaps it was that look alone that set the fire free and

ripping through her, or a heady combination of surreal, physical and maybe even spiritual pleasures. All she knew categorically was the power of that blinding-white moment of release when her eyes screwed shut, her head jerked back and a groan was torn from the heart of her.

Moments later, when the rolling waves grew fainter and further apart, finally she withered and lay, spent, on top of him.

She was drifting in some other perfect place when Nate gently eased her over and guided her onto her back. Then he was inside her again, working towards a second crescendo. Kneeling between her thighs, he reached behind, brought her knees up either side of him and continued to love her, hitting a spot that released a brilliant blue flame that tore through and engulfed her again.

She ought to have been mindless. Unable to think. And yet all the while one word swam through her mind. Not *scorching* or *orgasmic*. She couldn't shake it.

This was—*he* was—*magic*.

With Roxy lying worn out beneath him, Nate buried his face in her silken spread of hair, contemplating any likely way they could spend the entire morning wrapped around each other and enjoy more of this, when an odd sound drifted in through the screen covering the open window.

Laughter.

Easy.

Familiar.

A heartbeat after his eyes flew open, he drew up on his elbows, listened harder. At the same time Roxy stiffened then her head whipped towards the sound.

'Am I hearing right?' she asked.

That laughter came again and Nate smiled down into suddenly alert bright green eyes.

'Greg and Marla, chuckling.'

'Talking.' He sprang up, threw his legs over the side of the bed and, elated, smacked the pile of rumpled sheet at his side. 'They're back together.'

'Maybe.'

Frowning, he watched Roxy as she bunched the sheet up under her arms and joined him, sitting on the side of the mattress. 'People who are angry at each other don't laugh like that.'

'A ceasefire doesn't equate to resuming an engagement.'

He nudged her playfully. 'Pessimist.'

'Oh, I forgot. Of course you'd assume that true love conquers all.'

He looked at her sideways and got to his feet. 'No one can deny love is a powerful force.'

'You're the expert.'

She was grinning, that little dimple winking. But she was serious and he wouldn't rise to the bait. He grinned back.

'Well, y'know, maybe I *am* an expert.'

A bath towel, which had been placed at the foot of the bed, had fallen to the floor. He swooped and wrapped it around his hips before heading to the window for a look. Marla and Greg were strolling towards a dilapidated old sheep shed situated a short distance beyond the yard. He couldn't make out their words, but he read the body language. They were walking side by side, *close*, and glancing across at each other for long moments as they talked. Neither looked stressed. In fact, the pair seemed decidedly relaxed.

With the sheet draped around her, Roxy appeared beside him. She studied the scene for a thoughtful moment and finally grunted.

'Just as I thought.'

Squinting at the sunshine bouncing off the shed's tin roof, he asked, 'What do you think?'

'She hasn't forgiven him yet. Or not completely.'

'How could you know that?'

'They're not holding hands.'

His head coming forward, he looked harder and exhaled. Damn. She was right.

'They were the kind of couple who were always touching,' she said. 'His arm slung around her shoulders if they were sitting at home. Her leg sliding up his under the table when they went out to dinner. Always holding hands when they walked.'

'Be that as it may, they've made remarkable progress. By early afternoon, they'll be planning how to let everyone know the wedding is back on.'

Attention still on the couple disappearing around that shed, Roxy brought the sheet up higher under her chin.

'Maybe.' Her gaze dropped. 'I don't think you understand how hurtful a picture can be. It sticks in your brain even when you wish it wouldn't.'

He studied her profile and wondered. 'We're not talking about Greg's pictures from his buck's night, are we?'

She seemed to hold her breath before meeting his gaze again. 'The week after that engagement party, I happened upon a magazine shot of you. You were with a woman. A brunette. Some might consider her attractive. To my mind she looked like a bit of a tart.'

His mind wound back and in a few seconds he had the answer. 'That was no tart. Roxy, that was my sister.'

The sheet clutched higher around her throat but she shook her head. 'No. That's not right. You were *with* her.'

'I assure you, not in that way. Naomi's husband was interstate. I escorted her to an art gallery opening she didn't want to miss. If it makes you feel any better, I haven't dated a woman since that engagement party.'

Her eyes glistened and nose twitched as if she were battling a sudden rush of emotion. 'You haven't?'

'One of my other sisters, Ivy, thinks I'm a boring businessman with no social life.'

A smile lit her eyes. 'She *does*?'

He laughed, then wrapped his arms around her waist, brought her close and murmured against the warm shell of her ear.

'What say we do our bit to help the environment and save water by sharing a shower?'

In case she had any ideas about declining, he dropped his mouth over hers and moments later she was as pliant as warm putty.

'Just remember,' she purred, when he broke the kiss, 'making love for thirty minutes under a shower nozzle doesn't equate to conserving water.'

'I'll remember that if you promise not to work me into a lather.'

'I'll promise if you promise.'

Taking her hand, he led her to the attached bath and assured her.

He wouldn't promise anything.

Despite wanting to stay with her under the jets, Nate only kept Roxy in the shower for ten minutes, enough to froth her up and wash her down. And as he reluctantly turned off the water, in his mind he confirmed that these few days away were the best idea he'd ever hatched. He'd lost count of the times he and Roxy had made love and yet he still couldn't get enough.

Nothing he couldn't handle, of course. This was physical. Fun. He was a long way from falling down on one knee and pledging his heart. Especially now that Marla and Greg were back on track.

After he and Roxy dressed in jeans and tees, they stuck their heads out of the door and smelled breakfast, something salty and greasy, along with eggs and more scrumptious damper.

They ate in a huge old-fashioned kitchen, complete with yellowed vintage oven, scarred hardwood table and the cheerful company of Mr and Mrs Glenrowan. But there was no sign of Marla or Greg, although Mrs G let them know that it seemed some mice had raided the pantry and perhaps the other young couple had preferred a picnic for breakfast rather than sharing their company around the table this morning.

Over a warm cup of tea, Mr Glenrowan suggested a horse ride, so, after the dishes were cleared and Nate and Roxy fitted on suitable footwear, they made their way out front to see about galloping off down a wide-open plain. When they stepped into the sunshine, Mr Glenrowan had four horses saddled and ready. Greg and Marla were there too, chatting to each other while they waited.

Greg spotted them first and he put up a hand in greeting. 'You're joining us for a ride?'

Marla's smile was buoyant and a little contrite. 'Oh. Hi.' She threw a glance around. 'Great day, huh?'

'A beautiful day,' Roxy replied in an overly bright tone.

Mr Glenrowan was checking a gelding's girth strap. 'Who wants this one? He's good 'n' tame.'

Greg stepped up to a fine muscled animal with a glossy black coat and equipment that pronounced him a stallion. His palms smoothed over the horse's flank. 'I'll take this one.'

When all four were mounted, Marla said, 'Greg and I thought we might take a ride on our own, if that's okay.'

While Roxy exclaimed, 'Of course that's okay,' Nate grinned and mentally punched the air at the same time Mr Glenrowan gave instructions to them all.

'You'll find canteens in your saddle bags. Compasses too. It's a big place. Don't stray too far. And, each couple—you keep close together.'

Fifteen minutes later, after a head-clearing stint, cantering over a dusty red flat, he and Roxy brought their horses up to a slight incline.

'Where'd you learn to ride like that?' he asked, resetting his hat on his head.

'Pony club.'

'You'll have to show me your blue ribbon collection some time.'

Swaying in the saddle with the horse's gait, she grinned. 'I wasn't that good, I'm afraid. I only took lessons over a couple of summer breaks.'

'All you need now to really look the part is a pair of breeches and a dressage cap.'

'Don't forget the crop.'

'You'd use a whip to get a horse to move?'

She arched a teasing brow. 'I wasn't thinking about the horse.'

While he laughed, a few clicks of her tongue had Roxy's mount picking up pace and reaching the crest with his own steed close behind. Nate wasn't normally one to gape, but the majestic scene spread out before them was one of the most breathtaking he'd ever seen.

Fields of wild flowers, interspersed with eucalypt woodland, stretched out, covering, it seemed, every square inch of land from east to west. Pinks, golden-yellows, intermingled with patches of snow-white. The carpets of blooms, swaying in a sleepy breeze, looked so soft and smelled so fresh, both he and Roxy could only sit, speechless, and absorb one of nature's most striking canvases.

When Roxy's horse shook its head and blew a noisy breath out of her nostrils, still mesmerized, Roxy walked her mare down the slope and through the wide flowing river of petals. Overhead, Major Mitchell cockatoos squawked. With pink-tinged wings wide, they swooped before settling on tall branches to preen and flaunt their stunning crests.

He and Roxy stopped beneath the shade of a clump of trees. After dismounting, Nate made sure the horses were secure while Roxy roamed around, deep in thought as she ran her palms over a hundred different flower tops.

'I thought the Outback was supposed to be all red dust and dry grass.' Sighing, she surveyed the panorama, then lowered to flop back among the blooms. 'It makes me want to try something different,' she murmured, winding one arm around her head. 'Become a photographer or, better yet, a painter.'

Lowering beside her, he broke the stem of a soft pink flower and drew lines up and down her nearest arm with the petals.

'Or a florist,' he said.

'I do love a pretty bouquet.'

'How about flowers in your hair?'

He threaded the stem behind her ear and, looking into his eyes as if she might see her reflection there, she touched the decoration.

'My grandmother used to press flowers to keep the memories,' she said.

'That's sweet.' He pretended to clear his throat. 'I've, er, never been into flower-pressing myself.'

She laughed. 'Me neither. It seemed silly to try to keep your brightest memories alive by looking back on something all shrivelled and drained of colour. But lying here now, I understand why she did it. It's the connection…an association.' As she gazed up at the sky her expression took on a faraway look. 'Right now, it doesn't seem silly at all.'

She casually lay out her hand for him to take. Holding his breath, Nate took a mental snapshot of her lying among the petals, that flower in her hair, and, with only a flicker of hesitation, he lay down beside her and twined her fingers with his.

CHAPTER NINE

ON THEIR way back, Roxy and Nate stopped to check out an old windmill and a run-down shepherd's shack. They even enjoyed some Red Kangaroo spotting, staying well back and quiet while the roos lay sprawled beneath a tree, scratching themselves, or bounding off into a horizon that rippled with heat waves. Roxy had fed kangaroos in sanctuaries but seeing them looking so magnificent and at ease in their natural habitat was something she'd remember for ever.

When the sun blazed down almost perpendicular in the sky, they set their hats firmly on their heads, swung the horses around and cantered back. Later, as they were lashing reins over the homestead's front rail and drinking from their canteens to appease dry throats, Greg and Marla appeared, rounding a verandah corner.

When Marla saw them, a glowing smile lit her face. Leaning in, she spoke quietly to Greg, who acknowledged them too, and together they moved to join their friends, arms slung around one another's backs.

Nate spoke out of the side of his mouth. 'Mission accomplished.'

Roxy's chest tightened with relief and happy tears rose to sting her eyes. Seemed Nate was right. Those two truly *were* meant to be together, no matter what. They'd overcome that social media gaffe—those questionable pictures that had cut Marla to her core—and now they looked set to ride off into the marital sunset. Of course, Marla would need a gown—*the* gown—and Greg would have regained the personal strength needed to get back on board the Sparks Martin Steel train. Roxy released the pent-up air from her lungs. She could hardly believe this crazy scheme had paid off and everyone would find a happy ending.

But then she edged a look Nate's way and she held the spot where her stomach kicked. This short time spent here with him had made her feel so energized, different. Alive. And as he removed his Akubra and Frisbee-ed the black felt hat onto the verandah floorboards—with his strong bristled jaw thrust forward and a smile of victory lighting those incredible blue eyes—Roxy had to hold her jumping stomach again.

She'd gone into this plan reluctantly but also with blinkers removed. She'd known that, even when Nate felt so good pressed up against her, ultimately, succumbing completely to his charm would mean she'd pay a price one day. He'd made clear he wasn't interested in developing their relationship past 'fun' and 'now'. Problem was that being with Nate was *so* much fun, and not purely the sex, although that was stellar.

Riding beside him today—talking about each other's respective businesses, then his sister's plans for the anniversary party and onto how she'd always dreamed of having her own horse—she'd felt as if they *fitted*, like today's dry breeze through those windmill blades, or that surprise field of flowers and their rich red soil.

She might not *want* to think that way—feel that strongly—but there it was. She'd like to believe she wouldn't be upset if he never called again. But in her heart she knew she would be hurt, and deeply.

Dragging her from those thoughts, Nate took her hand and together they mounted the steps to join their friends.

Greg nudged his chin at the horses, drinking their fill from a vintage water trough. 'You really worked them.'

'How did your ride go?' Nate asked.

'Fabulous.' Marla caught Greg's gaze. 'But we've been back a while.'

'Occupying yourselves how?' Nate asked, without a hint of shame.

'Talking.' Greg studied Marla too. 'Making plans.'

'Or, more correctly,' Marla said, '*re*making them.'

Sensing the time was right, unable to hold the emotion back a second longer, Roxy came forward and flung her arms around her friend.

'I'm so relieved you two are all sorted. I've felt sick about the whole thing, particularly bringing you here.' Coming away, sighing, Roxy finished, 'But it's been worth it.'

Nate's grin was ear to ear. 'Hate to say it, but I told you so.' He stuck out his hand for Greg to shake. 'Congratulations— again.'

His brow furrowed, Greg studied Nate's hand while Marla pressed her lips together and shifted her weight to the other leg as if she was uneasy. She said, 'This isn't quite what you think.'

Nate's hand dropped. 'You've made peace, right?'

'Ready to exchange vows?' Roxy asked.

'We are back together—' Greg combed his hair back '—but we've decided to put on the brakes and take things slowly.'

'We've both had time to think,' Marla added.

'And we've talked a lot.' Greg exhaled. 'Thing is,

Marla still wants to go spend time with her brother in Los Angeles.'

'And Greg needs time to take over the family firm.'

At Marla's last remark, Nate's spine straightened and his nostrils flared. 'Take over? When did this happen?'

'My father and I spoke day before yesterday,' Greg said. 'He could see how lethargic I'd been. He told me that I needed direction and that he'd been planning the big handover next year anyway.'

Nate's chin lifted as he muttered, 'Son of a gun.'

'It feels right.' Greg growled at himself. 'I'm sorry I didn't let you know straight out the gate.'

Examining the parched timber near his riding boots, Nate thought a moment before a genuine smile graced his face. 'Like I said—' he held out his hand again '—congratulations.'

While the men shook and clapped each other's backs, Marla explained, 'We figured we'd try a long-distance relationship. If we survive that, we'll survive anything.'

Roxy wanted to be clear. 'So, no wedding?'

Marla squeezed her friend's hand. 'But we do want to stay on here with you two. Have some fun. Build some memories.'

Thinking of the flower Nate had threaded in her hair, the one she'd slipped in her shirt pocket and had pressed against her heart, Roxy found a smile and nodded.

'That'd be nice.'

It wasn't until everyone had hugged that she thought again of that gown, the contest and how now there was no hope. And on the heels of that came another recollection. One that zoomed large in her mind and sent a shower of icicles sailing through her middle.

Her gaze shot to Nate at the same time he blinked, frowned and his gaze shot to her. Without asking, she knew they were remembering the same conversation…his offer if all else failed…her acceptance if it should come to that.

To wear that gown herself and become Nate Sparks's wife.

Visible through their bedroom window, grey clouds laced with black rolled and rumbled in from the east. Glenrowan Homestead was due one heck of an afternoon storm, albeit nothing compared to the one brewing here inside this room.

'Don't be ridiculous.' Roxy dropped her riding boots in a corner, then crossed to enter the attached bathroom. 'Of course I won't marry you.' She closed the door.

Turning away from the sprawling view, he leaned against the window jamb, crossed his arms and spoke loud enough for her to hear.

'We had a deal.'

'I'm certain it wasn't written in blood,' she called back.

'If that gown doesn't make its walk down an aisle by the end of this month, any chance of you winning that contest is blown.'

'I wouldn't have won anyway.' She emerged from the bathroom. 'It wasn't meant to be.'

'You said the same about Greg and Marla.' Moving towards her as she sat on the edge of the bed to remove her socks, he conceded, 'They may not be exchanging rings but clearly they're a couple again.'

'A long-distance couple.'

'Who will phone and visit and, some time down the line, I believe tie that knot.'

'Because of that look they share?' Socks off, she stood and set her hands on her hips. 'That special ingredient.'

'That's right,' he said simply.

'But you and I don't share that-that-that…*thing*, right?

Because if we did, you would never suggest we get married, however good the reason.'

Her beautiful mouth was tight, pressed from pink to almost white. She was upset and he wasn't quite sure why. Their friends were reunited, although, no, not betrothed to be married again. But he'd stepped up to the plate to cover that contest problem with the gown. So why did she have her claws out? Wasn't as if he was doing *himself* a favour, going through with his end of the bargain.

He'd try to be logical. 'Roxy, someone needs to wear that gown in a wedding ceremony.'

She shook her head firmly. 'Wouldn't feel right.'

For Pete's sake. 'Forget about how it *feels*.'

Her jaw shifted a little and she sighed as if she'd never see another Christmas.

'I can't.'

Nate dragged a palm down his exasperated face. If *he* could think of this proposal in a purely pragmatic sense, surely she could. Certainly he didn't want to be a married man, but this was for show, for a limited season only. As she bundled up some delicates he tried again.

'The deal was we say the words and get an annulment.' Then, like a godsend, a light bulb flashed. 'In fact, what happens if we don't sign any papers? Then it won't be legal, binding.' *Genius.* 'Is there anything in the contest about that?'

A little colour returned to her lips. 'I'm not sure. I don't think so.'

'Then it's problem solved.'

'You really are a fix-it man,' she said, but she didn't sound as if she approved.

'All I know is that I don't give up easily.'

He'd seen what could happen if a man threw up his hands too soon. Bottom line, he wasn't his father. He was an achiever and, dammit, he was going to achieve and so was Roxy!

He thrust out his chest. 'So, are you in or out?'

'Out. And before you try to railroad me, just listen. Times are slow everywhere. To be honest, I was almost ready to close my doors, there were so many unpaid bills. But with Ava's deposit I'm almost up to date. And I managed to speak to Cindy briefly before our ride. I didn't want to tell you and jinx it, but she said she has another couple of ladies who are a bee's knee from sliding across some cash.'

He found an impressed face. 'That's sound great.'

She nodded. 'Being in the running was exciting, but the competition was *huge*. I was only ever chasing rainbows. You know that as well as I do.'

'Frankly, I think you have a good chance.'

'Thanks, but you know nothing about the industry.'

'I know how that gown looked on you.'

The image he'd stored in his mind floated up...flowing satin, cinched waist, beading that glittered like diamonds and made her look like a queen. You *bet* he thought she had a good chance.

But her expression was resigned, almost a mask, while her shoulder gave a jerk. 'Guess we'll never know.'

'You're being stubborn.'

'And you're feeling as if you need to pay me back for coming here, doing this for our friends. But you don't.'

He blinked and his arms unravelled. 'You are coming with me to my parents' anniversary do, aren't you?'

He knew this...*affair* wasn't meant to drag on. They weren't on the road to getting anywhere near serious. But he thought they'd settled that question. She was going to the party. Hell, he was looking forward to walking in, having her on his arm.

Before she could answer, her cell perched on the dressing table buzzed. Surprised, Roxy crossed and collected the phone. She inspected the ID and a sunny smile spread across her face.

'It's Cindy. Probably to say she has those other deposits.'

Roxy chirped out a greeting and Nate watched on as she listened more and more intently. Then her face slipped like syrup off a plate and Nate's midsection looped and tied in a double knot. When she turned as white as that china vase on the dresser, he held onto her shoulders for support.

Whatever the news, it wasn't good.

CHAPTER TEN

'WHAT'S happened? What's wrong?'

Roxy heard Nate's question. She tried to focus. But she simply couldn't.

A state of total shock. That was it. The world around her was receding. External noise was muffled, far away, unimportant. Her brow was damp and her head felt dangerously light. This couldn't be real. Not when things were beginning to come together for everyone.

Over a desert-dry throat, she rasped, 'I can't believe it.'

'Believe what?'

His grip on her shoulders tightened until the pressure points of each fingertip made her wince and she swam up from her daze.

'It's all gone bad.'

'For God's sake, Roxy, tell me. I'll fix whatever it is.'

A wave of dizziness whirled around her head and she slumped. 'I was too complacent. I should never have left.'

He inhaled slowly. 'Okay. From the beginning, tell me what happened.'

She met his intense gaze at the same time the churning in her stomach grew and crawled up to her throat. Lord, she was going to be sick. 'I need to get back to Sydney.'

'Come again?'

'The shop was burgled last night. They took near all

my accessories and trashed some gowns.' Hearing herself explain out loud made it all somehow real. More frightening. Repercussions were beginning to dawn.

'You don't have security?' he was asking.

'I cancelled when mounting bills got too much.'

'You must have insurance.'

'Some, but the premiums companies charge these days...some ask for more than I earn.'

He scrubbed a hand over his face. 'It's a blow, but you'll get over it. You have to stay strong. Focused.'

Yes. She should. Only one problem. She was numb and couldn't, *couldn't*, feel any other way.

He started to pace the room.

'Surely you still have customers—what about Ava and Violet, for instance?'

'They don't want the gown.'

He stopped dead. 'But they both loved that dress.'

'Violet found another one she loved more. Cindy said she was happy to leave half the deposit to compensate for the inconvenience. When Cindy tried to argue, Violet mentioned her daddy was a litigator.' She dragged her watery gaze up from the worn rug. 'I can't take a lawyer's daughter to court over a deposit, especially now.'

'Half a deposit's better than none,' he reasoned. 'And you have those other two gowns as good as sold, right?'

Nausea made her mouth water. Swallowing, Roxy shook her head. 'Yes. And no. Cindy got the deposits. Unfortunately, those gowns were ruined in the break-in.'

'Roxy, if you need money, I can help. You don't have to pay me back.' She imagined him drawing out a mental cheque book. 'How much do you need?'

'I don't want your money.'

'I can afford it. I've invested well over the years—'

'I'm not a charity case, particularly after...'

Her words trailed off, her gaze dropped and a heartbeat later he coughed out a humourless laugh.

'I'm not offering you money because we *slept* together, if that's what you think.'

'Would you offer if we hadn't?'

He frowned. 'That's…not a fair question.'

Who said anything about being fair?

'I appreciate the sentiment,' she said, bringing her case out from the cupboard, 'but I only want to get home. If you can organize something in a hurry, I'd be grateful.'

CHAPTER ELEVEN

THE next morning, Roxy walked into her shop, feeling as if she'd been away an eternity. The place was a mess. Some rows of gowns remained unsoiled, hanging pristine as she'd left them. One end of the glass counter was still intact, with sparkling accessories adorning clean satin beds. Nearer to the door, however, the glass was smashed and jewellery as well as other trimmings had been removed. To her soul, Roxy felt violated.

Making sure the sign read 'closed', she shut the door and demanded both rubbery legs carry her forward.

Her work. Her life. She dragged her gaze around as her stomach sank and her throat grew thick. How could people do this? She'd worked so hard and now she was as good as ruined. She'd have been better off working for a chain store stacking shelves. No risk involved there. No worry about overhead bills. No need to start again.

The salon's back door swung open and stylish tufts of blonde poked through. Cindy's expression brightened when she saw her company, but the smile wilted as her gaze swept the outside room.

'After the police left, I cleaned up best I could,' Cindy said, edging forward, her hands clasped tight before her.

And beyond her own grief and sense of despair, Roxy noticed her cousin's puffy eyes and realized she'd been crying. She reached for Cindy's hand, squeezed, and the younger woman's dark blue eyes brimmed.

'I'm so sorry,' Cindy said. 'You left me in charge and I let you down.'

'This isn't *your* fault. It's not anyone's,' Roxy grunted, 'except the brainless jerks who broke in.'

A tear slid down Cindy's cheek and Roxy drew her close for a big 'please don't worry' hug. When she was certain her cousin was okay, she patted her back a final time, then crossed to drift around the various racks, trying to piece together what was missing, what had been destroyed.

'I didn't think you'd want to open today,' Cindy said, 'so I kept the closed sign on the door.'

Roxy nodded but refrained from mentioning that, most likely, she wouldn't open again.

'You go home and take your mind off this.' Roxy crossed to the unharmed end of the counter. 'I have some phone calls to make.'

'I can help. Organize dry-cleaning, or put in orders for new jewellery.'

The burn of raw emotion backed up higher, pushing and demanding release. But Roxy bit down, held back. She didn't want to upset Cindy more than she already was. Besides, what good would tears do?

'Thanks.' She ran a hand over the counter. 'But I don't have the money for that.'

'Oh.' Cindy's petite shoulders stooped. 'Then what are you going to do?'

'At this point…' Roxy sighed. 'I don't really know.'

After Cindy reluctantly collected her bag and, with another heartfelt hug, said goodbye—she'd be in touch—Roxy stood behind the battered counter for a torturously long while, hoping that over-exposure might desensitize her pain. Didn't work. It seemed unreal that this time yesterday, she'd been floating on her own private cloud, horse-riding through a vast ancient wonderland. Lying in that field of flowers, she'd felt completely content. Blissfully satisfied.

Now...?

Rounding the counter, she entered the back room. In the far corner, Marla's contest dress hung high and safe, covered in light plastic. Roxy's heart lifted a little and a tiny smile hooked one corner of her mouth. At least she still had her dream dress. Although now, frankly, she had no idea what to do with it.

Give it away? Keep it for posterity?

She came closer and ran her fingertips over the plastic, remembering how divine the satin had felt against her skin that day. She'd never admit it out loud, but she'd thought it had fitted her better than Marla. Nate liked this gown too. He'd seemed certain it would do well in that contest.

She slid the gown off the rack, eased the petal-soft folds out of their cover. The beading seemed to smile up at her, telling her everything would be all right. As much as she wanted to believe, Roxy couldn't see that happening...

But she wasn't about to sit around doing nothing.

Steeling herself, Roxy put on a pot of coffee, got out the vacuum. A bucket and mop too. Needing inspiration, she slipped the contest gown over a mannequin in the main room, then set to work.

An hour later, she was sudsing up the mop when the bell above the door sounded. Curious, Roxy angled around. She was certain the sign on the door had been flipped to 'closed'.

Setting the mop aside, she came forward as a woman in her early twenties, with fire-red hair and several tattoos scaling the length of one arm and shoulder, sauntered in, looked around.

Smiling, Roxy wiped her hands down the sides of her jeans. 'I'm sorry, but we're not open for business.'

'I heard.' The younger woman headed towards the nearest rack and fingered some skirts. 'Your place got trashed.'

Roxy flinched at the word. 'That's right.' She frowned. 'How do you know?'

The woman flashed a wide grin that highlighted two front teeth with a gap you could stick a finger through. 'Police cars were parked outside yesterday. They were asking questions.' She sauntered around and fingered some more. 'I figured you might have a sale to get rid of damaged stock.'

'I really hadn't thought that far ahead. Right now I'm busy cleaning up and—' The woman was wandering towards the contest gown. Roxy sped forward. 'That one's for display only.'

'Wow…it's so beautiful. Teddy's eyes would fall clean out his head if I wore this.'

Roxy didn't want to be rude so she asked, 'Teddy's your boyfriend?'

'Fiancé. He proposed a few weeks ago. His folks live here. Mine'll drive down from Dalby.'

'I'm sure it will be a lovely day.'

'I've left off getting a dress. They're all so expensive.'

Roxy moved to stand a little in front of her gown. 'A lot of work goes into making a wedding dress.' A lot of hard work and affection.

'My sister said I could lend hers at a pinch. You know… something borrowed.' She studied the gown again, up and down and again, three times. 'So, you're not having a sale?'

'Not at this time.'

'You hire out?'

'I can recommend places that do.'

'I only have a week and a bit to get something organized if I don't want to borrow my sister's.'

'I'm sure you'll find something wond-er...' That last word stuttered and trailed as a cog in her brain clicked into place. Roxy cocked her head. 'What date is your wedding?'

'We didn't know whether to book Saturday or Sunday. Teddy's partial to Sunday. His family are religious.'

Sunday. The first of next month.

Roxy let out that breath and swept that crazy thought about slipping into that contest after all aside. 'Sunday weddings are lovely,' she made herself say.

'Except I insisted on Saturday. No sore heads at work the next day.' That gappy smile flashed again. 'So it's set. The thirty-first. The end of this month.'

CHAPTER TWELVE

NATE was pleasantly surprised when Roxy called and wanted to be filled in about arrangements for his parents' anniversary party. He said he could collect her at seven. He arrived at her house five minutes early. When she opened her door, looking incredible the way she always did, to say he was bowled over was a huge understatement.

Her gown was a shimmery silver that hugged rather than clung to her curves. Thin straps, low back, hair thrown up in a messy yet sophisticated style that not only left the elegant column of her neck deliciously available but also took her glamorous look to a whole other level.

She greeted him with a friendly smile and offered her cheek for a kiss. If only she knew how his brain had fogged up at the minute, she might have hidden behind the door for fear he'd carry her away and never bring her back.

Her arm linked through his, he escorted her down the path. The black leather interior of his sports car was a perfect foil for her dress.

'I'm glad you decided to come tonight,' he said, swerving the car from the kerb.

'I'm looking forward to it.' In the shadows, she shot him a glance. 'I was looking forward to seeing you again too.'

His heart beating faster, he changed up gears. 'Have you heard from Marla?'

'Not yet. Any word from Greg?' He shook his head and veered onto a road heading east. 'I'm sure she'll contact me before she heads off to California.'

As he routinely checked the rear-view mirror he nodded. Marla and Greg had made their decisions with regard to relationships as well as to work. He was disappointed Greg had chosen his father's firm over their fledgling enterprise. Then again, he understood. If his father had built a successful company, no doubt he'd be more than happy to take over the legacy, even if it meant compromising a little.

They'd done all they could for their friends. Now Nate was interested to hear what was going down in Roxy's life. Last he'd seen her, saying goodbye at the airport when she'd insisted taking her own cab to her shop, she'd been glassy-eyed. Shell-shocked. Tonight anyone would think she hadn't a care in the world.

'What about you?' he asked, telling himself to keep his eyes on the road, not on the shape of her legs through the skirt of that satin gown. 'How's the shop?'

He heard her sigh. 'I was devastated walking in. Cindy had cleaned up as best she could. I've spoken with the police but they have no leads and, without surveillance cameras, they don't hold much hope of tracking anyone down.'

'It's lucky Cindy wasn't in the shop at the time.' His grip tightened on the wheel. 'Or *you*, if we hadn't been away.'

'I thought the same.'

He waited a few beats. He didn't want to pry or bring down her mood. By the same token, they were only a few minutes away from his parents' house now. They'd have no privacy once they were through the property gates and among the revellers. He needed to know.

'Your gown…was it okay?'

'It was still there.'

'Not destroyed?'

'It was safely hung in the back room. Every bead is in place.'

'You must have been relieved.' He knew he felt relieved for her.

'After I sent Cindy home, I decided to clean up some more. I brought the gown out and fitted it on my favourite mannequin.'

'You have a favourite mannequin?'

'You'd have a favourite car or screwdriver, or whatever. I have a favourite life-size doll.'

He swung the car into his parents' street. A moment later, the estate gates appeared, as well as strings of different-coloured party lights. He could almost feel the vibration from a blaring sound system through the tyres.

He prodded. 'You put the dress on the mannequin, and...'

'I had a visitor—a woman who knew about the break and enter.'

His head snapped around. 'She knew who was behind it?'

'No. She saw the police the day before and enquired. She thought I might have a sale scheduled to shift damaged stock.'

He pressed a remote and the soaring gates opened. The uniformed man at the bottom of the long wide drive tipped his hat and waved them on. A giant marquee had been erected one side of the house. Guests were dancing, drinking, talking. He slowed the car down to a crawl.

'So, this woman,' he said, 'she was after something inexpensive.'

'I'm guessing she wasn't flush with money. She'd have loved to wear any one of the dresses.'

Nate swerved into the covered forecourt and uniformed

help swept up to park the car. When her door was opened, Roxy alighted and surrendered a long low whistle.

'Your mother's relative must have been loaded.' He'd told her the story about the inheritance. She cocked her head to take in the full length and height of the house. 'Nice mansion. Georgian style, yes?'

'A little over the top for my tastes,' he said, having eased out of the low-slung vehicle to stand in the fresh air too. They met at the front of the car where he straightened his black bow tie, then took her hand.

'This woman,' he said as they headed down a path lit either side by lakes of fairy lights, 'did she find a dress?'

'She didn't find a dress. She found *the* dress.'

'Ah. *Your* dress.'

'She fell in love with it. And guess when she's getting married.'

'Before the end of the month?'

'The thirty-first. I thought it had to be a sign.'

'That you should give this woman your gown and re-instate yourself in that contest?'

'With a nip here and there, it would fit her perfectly.'

The marquee entrance was a few strides away. People milling outside were studying the new arrivals. Word would spread like wildfire and any minute his parents would descend.

'Did she pay cash? Leave a deposit?' Enough to get Roxy back on her feet?

'I told her she couldn't have it.'

The sound of crystal flutes tinkling and occasional bursts of laughter seemed to suddenly grow louder. He pulled up so sharply, he jerked her arm. Had he heard right?

'You told her *what*?'

'I said no.'

Somehow he stifled a curse. If Roxy had driven him crazy before, this took the proverbial. She was being sentimental and she couldn't afford that luxury.

'I know you feel attached to that dress,' he said in a remarkably calm tone, 'but can't you put that aside to have a shot at something bigger?'

She laid a hand on his jacket sleeve. 'Can we talk about this later?'

He wanted to say no, he wanted to talk about it now. But she'd had a bad knock, and who was he to say what she ought to do from this point on? He was only the guy who couldn't stop thinking about her. Who'd kissed her, made love to her and wanted to again very much. When she'd phoned, he'd fought the urge not to jump in his car and speed over to see her straight away, but she'd been so distant since receiving news about that break-in. Although he wanted to support her, the bigger issue was not to crowd her. If she'd wanted to see him earlier, she'd have said.

So he'd shown some restraint, even containing himself when her lips had brushed his cheek in greeting tonight. All he asked was to know what she'd decided with regard to that gown, her salon. Whether she was ploughing on or shooting off in another direction.

Like, maybe to California with Marla.

Whatever she decided, he had no control. She wouldn't take a handout, wouldn't take him up on that offer to help get that dress back in its contest. He'd half thought about devising some plan to somehow work his way around one or the other of those options. But she didn't like him being creative where finding solutions was concerned. He'd simply have to put his faith in her choices. It wasn't as if they were a couple. Not a *real* one. Although tonight, he certainly felt proud having her walk alongside him.

In fact, he ought to simply enjoy the evening. Forget about the future. Have some fun as they had out west.

When Roxy changed the subject and said, 'Tell me more about these anniversary nights,' he put aside those other thoughts and concentrated on this evening.

'As you know, my parents' wedding anniversary has always been a big deal,' he said as they moved closer to the marquee, the borders of which were lit by flaming torches. Along the back stone wall, small groups gazed out over a harbour view, which included an illuminated coat-hanger bridge and iconic Opera House shells.

'Even when we were living on a shoestring,' he said, 'at anniversary time my parents managed to find money for a cake and gifts for each of us kids.'

'For the *children*?'

'All five of us.'

Her expression melted. 'That is *such* a beautiful thought.'

He spotted a middle-age pair trundling towards them and shored himself up. 'Here's the happy couple now.'

'Nate!'

His mother sailed up, looking like a diva in a stylish black satin trouser suit. She clenched his face between her bejewelled hands and brought him down to plant a rouged kiss smack on his lips. His father, as usual, was a step behind, looking debonair in a tux with a shimmering gold tie—clearly his mother's touch.

His mother gave her son a 'who's a naughty boy?' look. 'You should introduce us to this gorgeous woman, Nate, dear.'

'Roxanne Trammel, this is my mother, Judith, my father, Lewis.'

True to form, his mother brought Roxy close and gave her one of her famous python hugs.

Looking pleased too, behind his groomed silver beard,

his father smiled his eternally patient smile. 'Great to see you here, Roxanne. I'm glad he finally brought you home to meet us.'

Roxy was still recovering from the hug. 'It's lovely to meet you both too.'

Yes, his parents were sweet and wonderful—cloyingly so. At some point Roxy was bound to hear what a great catch he'd make and how eligible he was. As if he couldn't pick his own wife.

Which wasn't the reason behind bringing Roxy here tonight at all.

Hands laced before him, his father said, 'I believe you design wedding gowns.'

'Do you design other formal gowns?' his mother asked, taking in Roxy's dress. 'The one you're wearing is exquisite. It is your creation?'

'Thank you,' Roxy said. 'Yes, it is.'

'You should get your label on some catwalks,' his mother said.

'Unfortunately,' Roxy said, 'it's not as easy as all that.'

'Well, I'm going to pop down to your shop next week,' his mother went on, 'if you have something that will suit a woman my age, that is.'

'A person your age.' His father chortled. 'You're a classic beauty. Women twenty years younger don't compare.'

His mother cupped her husband's cheek. 'And people wonder why I married him.'

Nate noticed that Roxy didn't endorse his mother's suggestion to drop by the shop. Nor did she reject it, giving no clue as to whether she intended to carry on with The Perfect Dress or walk away.

'Do have some champagne and stay as long as you want,' his mother said a moment before her focus was diverted and she headed off. 'Oh, there's the Davidsons.'

'Have fun, kids.' His father winked and, following his wife, dissolved into the growing crowd of glittering guests.

A brow arched, Nate scratched his temple. 'So, what do you think?'

'I think you're very lucky. And they're lucky to have one another.'

Nate absorbed her sober tone, the sincerity sparkling in her eyes, and for the first time in his life he didn't wise-crack about his parents being joined at the hip or inwardly wish they weren't so damn saccharine and inseparable. Rather he recognized a shift at his deepest level. No one's childhood was perfect but if he had to do it over, he'd choose the same parents. The same memories.

Just as he wouldn't swap any of the memories he'd created with Roxy.

As he found them both a glass of champagne and she glanced around, her hips moving slightly to the music, the tightness in Nate's chest eased. The big introduction had gone well—neither parent had asked when the wedding would be, jokingly or not—and Roxy seemed to be enjoying the atmosphere. Was it that amazing dress or had she grown that much more beautiful these past days? She'd always been attractive in a unique way, but tonight her lips seemed fuller, her hair was shinier. Her subtle powdery scent was nothing short of drugging.

He raised his glass and made a toast.

'To the most beautiful woman here tonight. I second my mother's words. That dress is stunning.' Over the crystal rim, he murmured, 'You're stunning.'

An expression filtered over her face. A combination of pleasant surprise, appreciation...and something else. Something that made him half wish he were ready for 'serious'.

His attention skated to the dance floor and he made an executive decision. 'Let's dance.'

Swallowing a mouthful of champagne hard, she lowered her flute. 'Already?' Her gaze shot to the dance floor and the three couples gyrating to a seventies tune. 'Let's wait till more people are up.'

He removed the glass from her hand, set both on a passing waiter's tray and took her hand. 'I want to dance with you, Roxy.' Coming close, he nuzzled against her ear and a breath of heat blew through his blood. 'Aren't you curious to see how well we move together, swirling around without the water?'

She darted around a culpable look. 'You'll make me blush.'

He laughed. 'I hope so.'

Without giving her a chance to object again, he ushered her through waves of people to the floor, which was set outside beneath a blanket of twinkling stars. As they moved onto the temporary decking the song finished, the previously dancing couples wandered off and a slower, more intimate tune began to play.

Looking around, she nibbled her lower lip. 'Can't we do this later?'

'Like we'll talk more about that dress later?'

Words hovered on the tip of her tongue, but she wasn't ready to broach that subject yet. So she allowed him to curve a palm around her back and let him fold her right hand in his left. At the same time they began to move the main lights faded and a laser show, resembling softly falling confetti, filtered over the scene. Looking so masterful and handsome, Nate brought her deliciously near and soon the crowd seemed to fade as well.

With his gaze glued to hers, Roxy had to concentrate

not to reach up and brush her lips against the sexy half-grin lifting one corner of his mouth. By the time he twined their arms more and hers rested against his lapel, her feet weren't touching the ground.

Wondering if her smile reflected just how dreamy she felt, Roxy admitted, 'This feels good.'

His lips twitched. '*Very* good.' Indulging his natural skill, he danced her around in a tight circle. 'We should do this more often.'

Then something infinitesimal changed in his expression. A slight darkening of his eyes, the faint tightening of his jaw. But then that sexy grin returned and he urged her flush against him while the music wrapped around them and a sea of stars shone down.

With her cheek resting contentedly against his lapel, she was on another plane when the song ended and applause went up. Remembering where she was, Roxy blinked open her eyes and glanced around. An ocean of faces was beaming at them while couples whispered among themselves, Roxy guessed, about how perfect a couple they made. And for a long giddy moment, she had the strangest feeling—a flash—as if this were a rehearsal to a bigger event.

Nate's rumbling voice was at her ear. 'Is something wrong?'

'All those people looking on…' She gathered herself and sent a thin smile. 'For a moment I'd forgotten where we were.'

His frown eased before he brushed away a wave of hair floating against her cheek.

'At least everyone got a good look at your evening dress. You'll get enquiries.'

He was being genuine, but he was also digging for answers. He wanted to know if she intended to continue with the salon. But that would depend on what transpired tonight.

Five minutes later, a woman breezed up to them. Her dress was slimline, high-necked, covered in red sequins. Nate introduced them.

'Janelle, this is Roxy Trammel. Roxy, one of my younger sisters.'

'Roxy, I'm in love with that gown. Everyone's talking about it.' Janelle skated a look Nate's way, then stage-whispered, 'About the two of you too, actually.'

But Nate didn't appear to be listening. He was checking his cell's caller ID. He caught Roxy's gaze. 'Mind if I get this?'

She could tell by his expression it was important. 'Not at all. Go ahead.'

While Nate strode off to find a quiet corner, Janelle spoke to Roxy.

'A friend of mine expects to have the question popped any day now. Would you mind if I passed your name along?'

'Under normal circumstances, I'd love you to. Unfortunately, my salon was burgled recently.'

Janelle gasped. 'Much damage?'

'Quite a bit.'

'When do you think you'll be up and running again?'

'Can't say for sure. I should know more soon.'

'If there's anything I can do to help...' Her shoulders dropped. 'But of course, Nate would've already offered.'

Yes, he *had* offered, Roxy thought. But when push came to shove, would he come through?

Nate's other sisters gravitated over, one of them an effervescent brunette by the name of Naomi. They all five chatted as half a dozen songs played in and out. Each sister made her feel welcome and said she must come to another, less formal family get-together. Roxy longed to say she couldn't wait—she could easily see herself being friends with these women, particularly Janelle, who reminded her of a possum with her large chocolate-brown eyes—but she couldn't be presumptuous.

Only after she'd spotted Nate walking over did Roxy realize how much time had passed. The aroma of a delicious smorgasbord banquet being served inside the marquee teased her nostrils. It seemed dinner was served.

One sister—Ivy—announced they should find their respective partners and grab something to eat. The sisters snatched kisses and hugs from Nate as he moved closer. But on seeing his expression beneath the shadow and glow of party lights, Roxy felt a shiver pass through her. His smile was hollow. His gaze, preoccupied. When he finally joined her again, she felt unease ripple off him.

Rather than start a conversation, ask what she thought of his siblings, Nate swiped two drinks from a tray, passed one to her and skulled three parts of his down. His jaw was clenched, and a muscle beat rapidly and irregularly high in his cheek. What had happened? His face was so dark, she didn't want to ask.

'Guess the phone call wasn't good news.'

He exhaled, then knocked back the remainder of his drink. 'It's Saturday morning in Texas and Mr Nichols is clearing his desk.'

That shiver passed through her again. 'Clearing his desk?'

'His advisors have looked over my proposal, the figures. They're not convinced the investment's viable.'

Roxy didn't know what to say. He'd handled Greg pulling out, but now this? If she felt devastated by this news, how must he feel?

She touched his jacket sleeve. 'Are you okay?' He

blinked, looked down and then directly at her. Earlier he'd looked invigorated. Now suddenly he looked ten years older. 'We can leave, if you want.'

'I'm fine.' Then he raised his chin, rolled back his shoulders. 'I can get another investor.' His eyes narrowed on some imaginary distant spot. 'It's just a matter of pushing forward. Holding on.'

'I wish I could help.'

That seemed to bring him back. His gaze snapped onto hers, then he smiled. 'Like I want to help you with your situation.' He angled more towards her. 'You said we should talk later about your business, that dress. Guess it's later.'

'I don't know this is the right time.'

'Believe me. It's the right time.'

She took in the determined slant of his brows, the glint in his eye and tried not to think about the knot twisting in her stomach.

'There's no easy way to say this, so I'm just going to say it.' She took his hand. 'Nate, will you marry me?'

Nate heard the question. He let the words, the concept, sink in. For an instant he thought she was serious. That she was asking for his hand in marriage, and his heart skipped several beats before thumping back to life.

Then he remembered the dress. That contest that meant so much.

He eased out a breath and laid a palm on his heart. 'This is so sudden.'

Her lovely mouth twitched with a smile.

'That woman who came into the salon looking for a bargain, the one getting married on the thirty-first…I was on the verge of stripping the dress off that mannequin, wrapping it in tissue paper and exchanging it for nothing more than an invitation. After confronting the mess of that break and enter, not knowing whether I'd be able to stay open even another week, I felt I had no choice. At least this way, I had some kind of chance.'

'A *good* chance,' he reminded her, before taking her arm and leading her to a relatively quiet spot around the corner from the marquee and away from the constant thump of music. Climbing the step of an ornate white gazebo, laced with his mother's favourite scarlet-blooming vine, he indicated she sit and finish her story.

'You thought you had to take the risk,' he said as he lowered beside her. 'What changed your mind?'

'After that woman tried the gown on and we both agreed how well it suited, she asked if I could do a quick set of alterations. She wanted the bodice cut lower and the skirt made detachable so the dress could turn into a mini for the party afterwards. I told her the truth. The gown was a finalist in an international contest. If it were to remain in the competition, the gown couldn't be altered to that extent. She could have it free of charge, as long as she was married on the thirty-first and the gown was kept in its original state.'

From the far end of the estate, a stream of colourful lights whistled high into air. Next moment a blast of fireworks covered the previously dark sky. Another and another ignited, turning night into carnival day. Talking over the noise was impossible, so they sat tight and watched until the last celebratory star fell and distant applause and cheers rose up.

Roxy said, 'They'll wonder where we got to.'

'Don't worry about the party. What happened next?'

'The woman explained that her fiancé was in construction and he'd had this great idea. They should say their vows sitting in a bulldozer scoop and travel to the reception the same way.'

Nate's chin tucked in. 'Is that legal?'

'I wasn't thinking about the law. I was horrified for my dress. My jaw must have dropped so she hurried to explain that she'd insisted he have the scoop "cleaned good", that her dress wouldn't get caught on any spiky bits and that his pit bulls could forget about attending the after party. Apparently they go off on heavy metal music. Then she asked if she could light up in the shop. Of course she insisted she wasn't going to smoke in her wedding dress. At least not until after the ceremony.'

When Roxy shut her eyes and withered in the seat, he wrapped one arm around her shoulder and tugged her close. 'Not the sort of photos you want to remember that gown by.' Or to appear in an international magazine.

'I don't care about someone's personal habits or what kind of ceremony they chose. I've seen them all. But I couldn't shake the image of my beautiful gown mutilated by home alterations, grubbied by residual soil fill, mauled by a pack of hyper dogs and littered with crusted burn holes. I thought I could, but I just couldn't.'

Her shoulders felt cool so he tucked her in more against his chest until her cheek lay against his lapel and his fingers were stroking her perfumed nape. 'Which leads us,' he said, 'to this.'

'I reread the rules. I even spoke to an official. There's nothing that says a designer can't wear her own creation in a marriage ceremony as long as it happens by the thirty-first.'

Nate waited for the sweat to break on his brow, anxiety to wreath in his stomach. But he only felt a sense of relief. Both their professional enterprises had suffered a setback. Still he was far from finished, and it seemed Roxy wouldn't give up without a fight either. She was his kind of woman.

'Then it's settled,' he said as she straightened and his focus fell to her mouth, to the lips he'd missed so much. 'We'll be married.'

'What will your parents say?'

'Are you kidding? They'll be ecstatic.'

'Even when it's a scam?'

Grinning, he angled his head closer to hers. '*Scam* is a harsh word.'

'I didn't want to say con.'

'Let's go with temporary merger.' His lips brushed hers and a shower of pleasure that reminded him of the joy and colour of those fireworks shot through his veins. 'Or, maybe, a short-term fusion.'

When his mouth lingered lightly on hers, he felt her dissolve against him. She sighed. 'If you're sure.'

'I have one suggestion. We need a rehearsal.'

'Of our vows?'

'Of the kiss.'

CHAPTER THIRTEEN

AFTER that dynamite kiss, which lasted way into dessert, he and Roxy straightened themselves up, said their goodbyes to the clan and drove to her place, where Nate was invited to stay for the night. He stripped her of her evening gown, got rid of his tux, and that was before they made it to the bedroom. They made love and their coming together this time was different, more honest—at least it was for him.

As dawn spread its fingers up and beyond the horizon he decided he should at last let her sleep. If they were getting married in a week, arrangements would need to be made. Heck, he'd have to see her practically every night.

So he kissed her a final time, a long slow caress neither wanted to end, then he slipped away and drove home with the warm light of the sun rising behind him.

He grabbed a few hours' sleep, showered, then dabbled with the idea of speed-dialling her. Maybe she'd enjoy brunch somewhere nice by the water where they could discuss the arrangements for the coming event. He guessed she'd want to keep it low-key. Small.

As Nate poured a strong black coffee from the pot he scolded himself. Of course it should be discreet.

Still, his parents would be crushed if they weren't invited. His sisters and their partners too. In their minds, this might be the only time they'd get to see him say the words *I do*. He'd need to explain how the situation had come about, that he liked Roxy a great deal. Hell, he *respected* her. But neither of them was desperate for that larger commitment. He'd need to explain that the wedding was purely to help Roxy and her chance with that contest.

And organizing this wedding—whatever a groom was supposed to do—meant he wouldn't have so much time to dwell on Nichols and the fact he needed to find another investor if his plans for Sparks Steel were to go ahead. Lowering into a balcony chair, he sipped the tasty bitter brew—not nearly as good as Mrs Glenrowan's billy tea— and thought he really ought to do some work.

Thirty minutes later, he was still gazing at water taxies whizzing across the blue expanse of the harbour and thinking about Roxy, when the intercom buzzed. An instant of curiosity turned into hope. Maybe she'd decided to come visit. Then again, he'd never given her his address…

He was surprised when Greg's voice boomed through the speaker. 'Can I come up?'

'You and Marla haven't had another barney?'

'This visit's business.'

As he thumbed the button to allow his friend into the building Nate couldn't help but be optimistic. He'd always thought that once Greg's personal life was in order, his friend's professional happiness would follow. Greg had always felt under-appreciated in his father's firm. Perhaps after further consideration, Greg had decided he wanted back in Sparks Steel after all. Hell, he was welcome any time! As his own father had always said, a heavy load was made so much lighter when two people shared the weight.

When he let his friend in, however, Greg looked as if he'd been trying to cope with way too much.

'You look like crap.'

'I received an email, Nate. From the patent office. It

was stuck in my spam folder. They won't patent our best design.'

Nate waited for the punchline. For Greg to crack up and say he was joking. That he had, in fact, received news that everything had gone through smoothly, as expected, as they'd envisioned it would. But Greg's expression remained stern. And worse—filled with sympathy.

He handed over a printout of the email and Nate scanned the lines, his head growing lighter by the second.

Their steel roof, which incorporated its own unique approach to addressing insulation problems in Australia's harsh climate, had been dismissed on grounds that a similar idea was already in the pipeline.

Son of a bitch.

He'd thought he'd be in his own business within three months, but this, along with Nichols's pass…

'I know you had your hopes pinned on this design,' Greg was saying. 'Mate, I'm sorry.'

Nate wanted to screw the paper up and throw the useless wad—as well as a pile of furniture—against the nearest wall. He felt as if a sledgehammer had belted him in the gut then the head. The cave had fallen in on him. Where to from here?

Greg was still talking.

'I'm glad you have Roxy. Marla and I are so happy you two finally hit it off. When you have someone else to care about, the other stuff doesn't seem half as important. And I want you to know that we're always after great staff at PrimeSteel. If you want to make the move, consider it done. Just until you get this other thing off the ground, of course.'

Nate lifted burning eyes from the floor to meet Greg's commiserating gaze. And for one crazy instant, he wondered if he ought to take up Greg's offer. Maybe he'd be better off bowing to fate, marrying for real the woman who was so obviously right for him, and taking a secure position that would provide a pension and specified vacation time each year.

Greg's arm was twitching by his side. He raised a hand to lie on Nate's shoulder. Instead he rotated away. Greg knew him well. He couldn't abide an overload of pity.

'If you want to go for a beer later,' Greg said, 'give me a call.' He stepped out of the door. 'It'll all turn out in the end, Nate. The way it's meant to. You taught me that.'

As the door clicked shut Nate understood Greg was trying to help. Give him a subtle pep talk about treading water until the lifeboat arrived. But the waves licking his chin were rising and a school of sharks had begun to circle. He hadn't bothered looking into securing another investor. All he'd thought about today was Roxy and their sham wedding. With this latest setback how easy would it be to do as Greg suggested? Meld more with Roxy, opt for a less demanding career path, and surrender to the wider scheme of things. In other words, give up.

He'd rather slit his own throat.

Roxy received the call while flipping through an online catalogue for shoes.

The wedding planned for one week from today was only a means to an end—to see that her gown had its chance in that contest. Roxy was thinking 'garden wedding'. No need to try to book a church, which would be impossible at this late date, in any case. There were a number of celebrants she could contact to see if they were free, didn't matter what time of day. Six a.m. or ten at night, as long as the date requisite was met.

A bunch of wild flowers would make up her bouquet. She'd ask Marla to be her witness. She suspected Nate would ask Greg.

Appropriate lingerie wasn't a problem. What she did need was shoes, something Cinderella would swoon over.

Sitting with her laptop on her living-room couch, she dragged her attention away from a pair of satin pump wedges, with sparkling beads running from the top of the back seam all the way down the heel, to examine the ID on her cell's screen. Her tummy did a back-flip then she went warm all over. She'd hoped Nate would call today. Truth was after the glorious night they'd spent together, she missed him. *Lots.*

And as she thumbed the answer key a thought struck. They would need to get rings. Would he want matching gold bands? Of course there was no need for an engagement ring. Not unless he insisted.

'Are you busy?' he asked and her heart beat faster at the sound of his sexy deep voice.

'Actually, I'm working up a sweat choosing shoes.'

'Shoes?'

'For the wedding. If there's ever an occasion a woman needs a new pair of shoes, her own wedding must be it.'

She laughed, a light breezy sound. But her smile faded when only silence greeted her on the other end of the line. A slither of unease snaked up her spine.

'Nate? You there?'

'Roxy, I can't make it Saturday.'

She tried to decipher the statement. 'You'd rather we did it Friday?'

'What I mean is we need to find someone else to stand in. I'll be truthful. I can't do it. I know it won't be a real wedding, but I can't help thinking that if I watch you walk down any aisle in that dress and I say I do, that'll be it.'

'It?'

'My most important patent didn't go through. Greg kindly let me know I could work for him at his father's firm. Nice offer. I only have to put my tail between my legs and forget everything I've struggled to achieve thus far.'

Her lips felt like two loose rubber bands. She could barely get them to move. 'And going through with this ceremony—the one you suggested in the first place—would seal your fate?'

'I have someone else lined up. A great bloke I work with.'

She felt like crying. Dying. She couldn't believe he was doing this. She'd thought he'd changed. But he'd manipulated her again. Straight-out lied.

She ground out, 'How much did you pay him?'

'Don't worry about that. I just want to make sure this is all taken care of.'

Taken care of. Swept aside. Dismissed.

Last night she'd given herself to him as she never had before. Not only bodily, but with all her heart. All her soul. At one stage, as they'd lain among the moonbeams filtering in through her bedroom window, he'd kissed a loving line down one side of her neck, her shoulder, right down that arm finishing with the tip of each finger. She'd been overcome by the swell of emotion—a powerful awareness she couldn't deny. In real time they hadn't known each other long, but in a way that mattered more she'd known him all her life.

He made her feel happy. Whole. He made her feel *love* like she hadn't believed in. As his lips had grazed hers very early this morning and he'd gently closed the door she'd felt certain about them. She might as well admit it.

She'd fallen in love. And a tiny hopeful part of her had whispered that he might just have fallen in love with her too.

Again and again she'd told herself this wedding wasn't the real deal and yet, the way he'd spoken and behaved last night, she'd thought deep down that maybe Nate wanted it to be. And now he was telling her she needed a replacement?

She wanted to argue. Slap his face. Of course she knew this make-believe marriage was only a means to an end, a way to keep her gown in that contest and her hopes to keep her salon alive. But as the silence stretched and she felt Nate's determination—his fear—the need to object, defend, persuade, disappeared.

Hadn't she told herself one day she'd pay a price? She'd fallen for a man who had vowed never to fall under a woman's spell. No, she wouldn't argue with him. Even feeling as if her insides were being torn out, she wished him well.

As long as he never dared try to see her again. If he did, she swore she'd tear him apart.

But she didn't want to say goodbye looking vulnerable or needy. Because she wasn't. In fact, this episode had made her a thousand times stronger.

'Actually I've had second thoughts too,' she told him, her tone as sincere as she could manage. 'I know rules are rules but when all the other contestants' gowns will be part of a genuine ceremony, where a couple who are committed beyond all else pledge to be there for ever for one another no matter what, I'd feel like a cheat.' And the slam-dunk. 'Guess dishonesty really isn't my deal.'

Another long silence. But she wasn't about to play that game either, batting the ball back and forth, telling herself if she could keep it in the air long enough she just might win.

As a jet of emotion threatened to erupt her grip tightened on the phone and she forced out the words.

'Goodbye, Nate.'

'Roxy, wait. Maybe we should have a drink. Talk about alternatives.'

'I'd rather not.'

'I was only trying to be honest with you.'

She set her jaw, took a breath, cursed her feelings.

And cut the line.

CHAPTER FOURTEEN

'I DON'T know why you don't get rid of this clapped-out bucket of rust.'

Standing in his parents' four-car garage, Nate leaned against a pristine workbench and told himself to count to ten. He loved his dad, but, Lord above, the man infuriated him. With the money they'd inherited, he could afford a Porsche and, to be fair, his parents did drive a very nice locally made sedan. But his father insisted on keeping this relic from the past. A bomb. He never drove it, just tinkered as he did now, hunched over the engine, checking and pulling at bits. A waste of time.

Lewis Sparks raised his head from under the hood. 'Rust bucket? This body's as perfect as the day it came off the line. Besides, it was my first car. We've had some good times together.'

Nate wanted to block his ears. 'I've heard the story about the night Grandad caught you necking and banned Mum from seeing you again.'

Through that neat silver beard, his father's grin appeared. 'She sneaked out late at night. We dabbled with the idea of eloping.'

'I don't want to hold you up. I just need that number.' He'd already explained ten minutes ago when he'd first arrived. He wanted the number of the patent lawyer his father occasionally enjoyed eighteen holes with.

'You're having trouble with your idea?'

'I'd rather not go into it.'

His father found a rag, wiped his hands thoroughly, then changed the subject. 'Your mother and I liked your date the other night.'

Pushing off the dusty workbench, Nate held up his hands. 'Before you ask when you'll see her again, she and I have called it quits.'

'Oh.' His father nodded slowly. 'I see. Your mother and I—'

'Dad. Sorry. I really don't have time.'

'Sure. Fine.' His father stuck his head back down near the bomb's engine. 'I'll get Roger's number after I check this battery.'

'I thought you put a new battery in last month.'

'One of the cells was flaky. One flaky cell and the whole caboose is let down. It's not pretty like a flash paint-job or a shiny set of rims, but a good battery's what keeps a car going strong.'

He fiddled with cables, then straightened and rubbed smudged grease off his hands on that rag again; Nate recognized it as a shirt from twenty years ago.

'Mind turning her over, son?'

Grabbing the time on his watch, Nate suppressed a growl. He'd wanted to dash in and out. He'd have got the number over the phone if someone had answered when he'd called. Apparently his mother was out visiting one of the girls. His dad, as usual, had been tucked away in this sanctuary where he kept his toys—this beat-up old Holden and a tin boat he'd had since his youth.

Nate threw open the driver's side door. He would start the car, then they could go inside, get that number and he'd see what could be done about getting another hearing for his patent. He'd already poured a river of money into fees. This was not a little matter.

Dammit, he would *not* roll over now.

Pressed into the smelly vinyl seat, he rotated the key and the V8 roared to life. His father lowered the hood, which snapped into its catch with a crashing boom.

'I'd rather have a dozen of these than one European sports car with a dodgy engine.'

'I have a European sports car, Dad, and the engine runs just fine.'

His father thought that over and tossed the rag aside.

'Guess I'm just easy to please.' The older man's attention shifted, as did Nate's. They both peered out as a car drove up. His mother's. But another car followed and another.

'Hey, your sisters and kids are pulling up too. I'd better warm up the barbie.' His dad started out and hooked an arm. 'Come say hello.'

Nate was about to say again he was rushed. But his father looked so happy to have the family together... Nate mustered a smile and said he'd be out in a minute.

Nate watched as everybody hugged. Didn't matter if they'd seen each other three months ago or yesterday. No one escaped a python squeeze from Mum. Dad must have mentioned his eldest was in the garage. All the women looked his way and various gestures and pleadings called him out. But Nate shook his head, his hands. He wasn't ready yet.

So he sat in that smelly old car watching his family meander up the path, into the house, and as they disappeared through the back door Nate found himself wondering...

Why am I so different?

They always seemed so content. So easily pleased. But he was enquiring. Restless. A weak link.

The flaky cell.

He'd told Roxy he was nothing like her father and yet he'd ignored her feelings, lied to her, let her down.

For as long as Nate could remember, he'd been drawn by the notion of finding his own way, and yet, sitting out here all alone, he'd never felt so lost.

CHAPTER FIFTEEN

'I WAS told I'd find you here.'

Every fibre in Roxy's body locked and then trembled as that deep sexy voice rumbled down at her.

The day was grey and cold, but she'd needed to get outside and hopefully be productive while she was at it. Rugged up in a red trench coat, she'd found a place in a nearby park to spread out a light blanket and play around with a few sketches for some new dress ideas.

Now she set her pencil aside and, swallowing a calming breath, forced herself to peer up.

Standing with his hands thrust deep into their overcoat pockets, Nate Sparks towered over her. A lock of dark hair fallen on his forehead bobbed with the breeze. His gaze was piercing, holding hers with an intensity that made her quiver. In that moment, it all came rushing back...the way they'd splashed around and made love in that creek. How they'd happily gone without sleep to spend every available minute pleasuring one another in that big soft bed in the bush.

Now, when he moved closer, she instinctively felt her heart lift and reach out to him. But she didn't jump up and into his arms, although, God help her, she wanted to.

'There's a lot happening at your shop today.'

She kept her voice even, her reply short. 'It was time for a big sale.'

His brow pinched. 'How much are you getting rid of?'

'As much as people want to buy.'

'Your cousin seemed to be holding down the fort well enough.'

'I have complete faith.'

Clearly she needed to resize, regroup and, hopefully, start building again. But she didn't have the heart to be there, watching the gowns she'd spent so much time and loving effort on sailing out of the door for a song.

He nudged his chin at the sketchpad. 'What are you doing?'

'Getting inspired.'

'For new gowns.'

'A new life.'

Digesting her words, he nodded slowly, then thought for a long moment before speaking again.

'I want to apologize.'

Her heart jumped but she kept her mask cool. 'Whatever for?'

'I let you down.'

'Yeah. Well.' She shrugged. 'Nothing I haven't coped with before.'

'I'm not like your father.'

'You're certainly not like yours,' she bit back. 'You don't know the meaning of the word *integrity*.'

She was glad he'd called that day and put an end to it all.

'I know I hurt you,' he said. 'I hurt myself too.'

'Let me dig out a tissue.'

'There's still time for that wedding…if you haven't found a replacement.'

Collecting her pencil again, she sketched a few lines.

'I'm over the contest. I did my best. Time to move on.'
Speaking of which…

Grabbing her bag, pad under one arm, she pushed to
her feet and, fighting a cold wind, headed for the car park.

His voice boomed over her head. 'I'm not ready for
this to end.'

Anger and hurt clogging her throat, blurring her vision,
she called back, 'Too bad.'

The determination in his voice hit her again.

'Dammit, Roxy, I love you.'

Her blood stopped pumping as every kind of emotion
funnelled through her centre and then jetted up to fill her
face with scorching heat. Her head was swimming, her
world tilting. He *loved* her. She hadn't expected that. Not
for one moment.

Needing something to hold onto, she angled carefully
around. She swallowed but her words still came out a
hoarse whisper.

'I mustn't have heard right.'

'I'll say it again. *I love you*, in a way I never thought
possible—' he gave a weak lopsided smile '—even with
parents like mine.'

She wanted to ask if he was teasing her. After his
previous stand, whether he truly meant it. But then she
remembered her father declaring his love and her mother's replies… 'Do you, Tom? Do you *really*?' …and the
merry-go-round would start turning again. Even as a girl
with no experience, Roxy had thought her mother a fool.
She'd vowed never to sound that desperate. Be that gullible.

His brows knitting, Nate stepped closer. 'You don't believe me.'

Her voice, and heart, broke. 'Doesn't matter if I believe
you or not. Nothing in this world could convince me to

get tangled up with you again. So, please—*please*—just leave me alone.'

When she turned again, telling herself to keep walking no matter what, he overtook her and blocked her path. She wasn't about to rant and try to push her way around him. Instead she stood calmly, pinning him with her best death glare even while her very soul begged her to crumple and surrender.

He drew something out of his overcoat pocket. Roxy glanced down. Between his fingers, he held a fine silk thread.

'Could you hold this?'

As his strong tanned hand came forward, her mouth tightened. 'I won't play your games—'

'Roxy, just do this one thing.'

With those gorgeous blue eyes glittering over at her, Roxy remained firm for another five full seconds. Then she huffed out a breath, rearranged her sketchpad and held the damn thread.

From his other pocket Nate retrieved something else. A heartbeat later a shining ring slid down the line and into the palm of her hand. Her eyes wide, she swallowed a gasp and automatically brought the surprise near. It was an engagement ring…a solitaire, clear and bright.

She imagined how it might look on her hand. How her gaze might drift to that finger time and again to make sure it was real and as beautiful as she thought. She thought of how her friends would swoon over the diamond, then envisaged the matching gold band that would slip on in front. Nate stepped into the space separating them and his arms went out to bring her near.

But before he could press her close, she remembered how gutted she'd felt when he'd dumped her cold, and how many apologies she'd heard in her life. A marriage proposal wasn't a cure-all. In fact, given everything he knew about her, it was an insult. Stronger, she dropped the ring back in his pocket and, breaking inside, braced her shoulders and walked away.

She wished he could mend the wound, make her feel differently, but there simply weren't enough words; there was nothing he could do.

Her pace picking up, she saw her sedan appear through her blur of tears at the same time a familiar sound vibrated through the air. She stopped, turned and, sure enough, a horse was nodding its head, pawing the grass. But not just any horse. She was pure white, even the saddle and bridle and reins. But that wasn't all. Walking up to meet it was another horse, black and large, his glossy mane flying in the wind. For a flash of a second Roxy forgot how much her chest was aching. The sight of those beautiful animals brought back so many memories...of her and Nate cantering over Outback planes...of her pony-club days, before she'd become interested in fashion and had only ever wanted her very own horse.

She soaked up the sight for as long as she dared—she didn't want Nate to think she was hanging back waiting for him—but before she had time to hitch up her sketch-pad and carry on to the car, something else unusual caught her eye. A well-dressed lady carrying an opened gold-leaf book was walking up to the horses. If this had been any other day, any other time, she'd have stopped to see what happened next.

Of course the first thing to cross her mind was a wedding. A romantic unique ceremony on horseback with that lady, dressed in a pale pink suit, overseeing the exchange of vows. But they were missing the guests and, more particularly, a bride and groom. Perhaps it was a photo shoot or publicity stunt or—

The notion popped in her brain, like a balloon bursting, but as soon as it appeared she shunted the idea aside. She was being ridiculous. That scene had nothing to do with her, with Nate's proposal, or that amazing diamond-and-gold ring.

When a man in a morning suit appeared, collected the horses' reins and began to lead them over, Roxy felt the edge of reality shift and everything but those horses and the memory of Nate's declaration of love faded into the background. But she couldn't believe this was happening. She didn't want to accept that Nate had set this all up. This all might be a coincidence and he'd already left and she was just standing here looking like...

Looking like a fool.

Shoring herself up, she swallowed down ever-rising emotion and prepared to continue on to the car. But a light grip on her arm held her back, and in an instant her entire body turned cold then inexplicably hot. Fighting the giddy spin, she let herself be angled around, then looked up and into Nate's loving eyes.

'The white mare is yours,' he said.

Her voice trembled and tears welled. 'Mine...?'

'To keep. The woman waiting over there—' he tipped his head and Roxy watched the lady nod and smile in greeting '—she'll do the honour of marrying us. I brought your gown with me—it's in my car, if you want to wear it.'

'Nate, no.' She shook her spinning head. 'I haven't said yes.'

His lips twitched. 'You don't think I'd let that stop me.'

He pressed her close and her sketchpad dropped to the ground. 'This is where I'm meant to be, what I'm meant to do. Be with you. Adore and love you every day for the rest of our lives.'

She worked to swallow against the lump growing in

her throat. 'Nate, you wouldn't tease me about something like this. You wouldn't, would you, if this were just some act…if it weren't true?'

Setting his hands on her shoulders, he rested his brow against hers. 'Tell me, Roxy. Say you love me too.'

Tears, built in her eyes, were sitting, ready to spill. She took a shuddering breath, but she couldn't say the words. She wanted to believe so much, and when she thought of his parents, rather than hers, it actually seemed almost possible.

'You've shown me so much, Roxy. Taught me so much. Things I didn't think were important but ends up are the most important of all.' His committed gaze roamed her face. 'I love you. Only and for ever you.'

She felt so weak, helpless and, at the same time, so empowered.

'I want to cherish and protect you,' he went on. 'And I know we'll be happy because I can feel it, Roxy—' he put her hand to his chest '—right here.'

A tear escaped, rolling down her cheek. 'This is what you were most afraid of,' she warned him. Falling in love. 'Aren't you even a little scared?'

'Only in a good way, like when you start a new adventure. One that will last two lifetimes.'

With his eyes glistening into hers and his grip on her upper arm holding her tight, she eased out a breath and gave in to his will. To his faith and their love.

More tears fell, rushing down her face, curling around her chin. She hadn't thought it was possible, but he'd done it. He'd stripped her of her doubt. And she believed, believed with all her heart.

For some there really was a happy ending.

Her mouth wobbling with a smile, she choked out, 'I love you, Nate. You know I do.'

His chest expanded, then he let out a long full breath. 'And I'll never forget it. Never ever take you for granted.'

As her arms threaded around his neck and his head lowered again a collective cheer went up. Roxy's breath caught as she turned her gaze towards the noise. Emerging from behind various trees were Nate's mother and father, his sisters, their husbands and a flock of children. Cindy and Marla were there too, waving, while Greg shook combined victory fists above his head. And there was another person, dressed in chiffon, a gardenia corsage pinned to her bodice. Her throat backed up with her emotion, Roxy croaked out, 'You brought my mother here?'

'All we need now are the bride and groom.'

When, breaking into a bigger, even brighter smile, she nodded, he swept her up in his arms and carried her off to those guests, to their wedding and what was destined to be a blissful new life.

EPILOGUE

LUNGING, Roxy snatched up the hands-free before the phone rang a third time.

Usually at this time of day she turned the volume off rather than down and let whoever it was leave a message. But she was expecting an important call, one she hadn't told a soul about…not even Nate. Thinking of how much their lives might change after this conversation, she felt a little faint. But, God knew, there was no going back.

After she'd answered with, 'Mrs Sparks speaking,' a sophisticated female voice replied.

'I'm glad we're finally able to talk. You're a hard woman to pin down.'

'Well, life's busy, business is booming and…' Roxy paused. She thought she knew who was calling. Now she stopped to ask, 'I'm sorry, who is this?'

'My name is Harper Valance.'

Ms Valance went on to explain that she worked for a well-respected pregnancy and parenting magazine. Her position was managing editor. Butting a shoulder against the nearby jamb, Roxy took it in and gathered her thoughts.

After their wedding day, when she'd worn that special gown, she'd made the contest deadline but had neither won nor come a place. She hadn't been upset. There'd been so much to occupy her mind and her time.

When the required time had passed, she and Nate had signed the appropriate papers, making their marriage legal and binding, and this past year she'd switched from designing bridal wear to having the best time creating her own maternity line. Her shop had been relocated closer to the home she and Nate had purchased together near the harbour, and her affordable outfits were gaining popularity. Clients had suggested opening in other major cities or that she launch an online shop. The Internet certainly made the world a smaller, more convenient place.

Roxy was rapt by the response. She'd begun this new venture with nothing more than a fabulous challenge in mind; she wanted to help mothers-to-be feel and look that much more beautiful. Now, given this phone call, it seemed that word had spread further afield than she'd thought.

Turning, Roxy leaned the other shoulder against the jamb and looked into the adjacent dimly lit room. 'Your magazine wants to do a spread on my line?'

'Actually, we'd like you to consider heading a column for us,' Ms Valance said. 'I've followed your blog "Family Blessings" since your wedding. Congratulations on the new addition, by the way. You and Mr Sparks must be thrilled.'

As her chest warmed and a grateful smile spread across her face Roxy studied the peaceful form bundled up in a cot positioned in the far corner of that quiet darkened room. Her precious baby was sleeping soundly, although Hayley Jane would need to wake soon for her bath and dinner. With Nate's dark hair and startling blue eyes combined with a smile that melted her parents' hearts, their daughter was a delight. Every day was an adventure, filled with emotions so intensely satisfying, Roxy couldn't imagine feeling more content.

Ms Valance was explaining, 'We're interested in your

experiences as a businesswoman, designer, seamstress, wife, mother. Woman. Frankly, I love the energy of your blog posts. Given the healthy number of comments you receive, I'm not alone.'

'That's a wonderful offer, but the truth is I'm rather time poor at the moment.'

'Let me explain.' Ms Valance took an audible breath. 'With your permission, we'd love to use backlist excerpts from "Family Blessings". Of course, we'd also be open to view pieces you might like to create whenever a more, let's say, *exclusive* muse strikes. You have a lot to say and, I'm sure, a lot more to share.'

When Hayley stirred in her cot, Roxy quickly and quietly thanked Ms Valance for the offer. She needed to talk with her husband and would get back to her soon. Setting the phone in its cradle, she had to smile. Once, not long ago, she'd ached for the chance to boost her profile. Make a big career splash!

Now?

Her priorities had changed. *Life* had changed and, in a thousand ways, for the better.

The phone rang again, and this time the caller was the person Roxy had expected. As she ended the call a couple of minutes later the baby stirred again and Nate swept into the room. He stopped to steal a lingering, loving kiss and rub the tip of her nose with his before heading into the nursery.

'I heard the baby squeak,' he said. 'I'll get her.'

Hayley wasn't near fully awake yet, so Roxy held her husband back. His curious look faded into an adoring expression that confirmed every remarkable thing she knew about him and their incredible life together. Reaching on tiptoe, she pressed in close and wound her arms around his neck.

'You're home early.'

'Dalton Majors can look after anything that crops up.'

'The new second-in-charge is working out well, then.'

'Dalton's sharp, decisive.' He cocked his head. 'I didn't think so at the time, but, in hindsight, it was best Greg didn't get on board. This was always far more my project than his.'

She wound herself closer, enjoying her husband's hard heat and divine masculine scent. 'And you didn't need that Mr Nichols or his money either.'

He'd needed to take that leap of faith and do what *Nate Sparks* wanted to do. After that initial hitch, the problem with his patent had been rectified and his company was flourishing, as Roxy had known it would.

As if he'd read her mind, he murmured close to her lips, 'What I need is to make sure you and Hayley are happy, every day, in every way.' He flicked a glance towards the nursery before his palms, hot and steady, slid up her sides. 'I think she'll sleep a while longer.' He leaned in to growl playfully at her ear. 'I could use a lie down too.'

As his mouth slanted over hers Roxy sighed and dissolved.

When they came together—when they made love— the joining was always amazing, and with each passing week, with every passing moment, the love they felt for each other only grew. In her soul Roxy knew this was for ever. Not because of the Sparkses' family 'curse' but because two people could be lucky enough to overcome hurdles from both past and present. Two people could fall and *stay* in love when that unique prize was paramount to them both.

As the kiss slowly broke and Nate's attention turned to savouring the sensitive slope of her neck Roxy fought the sizzle of desire to find the wherewithal to ask, 'Don't you want to know who was on the phone?'

'Mmm…' He found the zip at her back and tugged. 'Later.'

Roxy grinned. He'd want to know now.

'The other day I went to the doctor's to confirm a test I'd taken.'

He stilled. She felt his heart thumping near hers before he pulled back. His expression was anticipation, happiness, disbelief.

'You're pregnant? Again?'

He brought her close, hugged her tight. She knew him well enough to imagine the emotion prickling behind his eyes. Then, as if he'd had a startling thought, he pulled back again.

'Why didn't you tell me sooner?'

She drew down a breath and tried to explain.

'Because something felt…*different*.'

His jaw clenched as he gripped her upper arms. 'Are you all right?'

'I'm great—now that I know the results of the scan and everything's fine.' Her hands cupped his handsome curious face. 'We have *three* babies, Nate. Three little lives growing here, inside of me.'

With an ever-growing look of astonishment, he covered her tummy gently with a big warm palm. She watched his throat work. Saw his chest expand on a deep breath. He blinked, gazing into her eyes, and croaked out a question.

'Three?'

Feeling elated, relieved, she laughed. 'That family curse—' *blessing* '—is particularly potent in your case.'

'Our case.' Beaming, he gathered her close again. 'This was a group effort. And it'll be a group effort in parenting.'

Her lips twitched. It would *need* to be.

'Maybe we ought to go back to being extra careful about contraception after this delivery,' she said.

'That's up to you. All I know is…' His strong fingers scooped through her hair and held her head firmly so he could look deeply into her brimming eyes. 'God, I love you. I've always loved you.'

He swept her up into his arms and was striding off towards their nearby bedroom when the baby mewed and they both looked back. Hayley was wide awake, kicking and arms out, ready for cuddles.

Carefully, Nate set his wife back on her feet, and as they moved towards their six-month-old daughter he said, 'It's going to be busy around here.'

At the cot, Roxy lifted a giggling Hayley up. 'And noisy.'

Nate screwed up his nose at a suspicious smell. 'And messy.'

Roxy snuggled both of them close. 'Darling, it's going to be heaven.'

Nate's mouth found hers, and as the caress deepened Roxy couldn't help but be struck by an extraordinary, wonderful fact. Every time they kissed, every time he drew her near, the emotion touched a new and beautiful place—a place she hadn't quite known existed until that moment. And each time it happened—every time she was lifted up—the words she now lived by bubbled up in her mind and her heart.

This was the deepest kind of love.
Theirs was the best ever life.

* * * * *

MODERN™

INTERNATIONAL AFFAIRS, SEDUCTION & PASSION GUARANTEED

My wish list for next month's titles...

In stores from 19th October 2012:

- ☐ A Night of No Return – Sarah Morgan
- ☐ Back in the Headlines – Sharon Kendrick
- ☐ Exquisite Revenge – Abby Green
- ☐ Surrendering All But Her Heart – Melanie Milburne

In stores from 2nd November 2012:

- ☐ A Tempestuous Temptation – Cathy Williams
- ☐ A Taste of the Untamed – Susan Stephens
- ☐ Beneath the Veil of Paradise – Kate Hewitt
- ☐ Innocent of His Claim – Janette Kenny
- ☐ The Price of Fame – Anne Oliver

Available at WHSmith, Tesco, Asda, Eason, Amazon and Apple

Just can't wait?

Visit us Online

You can buy our books online a month before they hit the shops! **www.millsandboon.co.uk**

1012/01

Special Offers

Every month we put together collections and longer reads written by your favourite authors.

Here are some of next month's highlights— and don't miss our fabulous discount online!

On sale 19th October   **On sale 2nd November**   **On sale 2nd November**

Save 20% on all Special Releases